Henry Augustus Rawes

Homeward

A Tale Of Redemption. Second Edition

Henry Augustus Rawes

Homeward
A Tale Of Redemption. Second Edition

ISBN/EAN: 9783337342753

Printed in Europe, USA, Canada, Australia, Japan

Cover: Foto ©Andreas Hilbeck / pixelio.de

More available books at **www.hansebooks.com**

HOMEWARD

BY

THE REV. FATHER RAWES, O.S.C.

Φωνᾶντα συνετοῖσιν

Pind. Ol. II. 15s

𝔖𝔢𝔠𝔬𝔫𝔡 𝔈𝔡𝔦𝔱𝔦𝔬𝔫

LONDON
BURNS, OATES, & COMPANY
17 AND 18 PORTMAN STREET, AND 63 PATERNOSTER ROW
1873

PRINTED BY BALLANTYNE AND COMPANY
EDINBURGH AND LONDON

I HAVE WRITTEN THIS BOOK

FOR THE DAY OF THE RESURRECTION,

AND THE MEETING OF THE BRIDEGROOM AND THE BRIDE

AMONG THE LILIES AND POMEGRANATES

OF THE PARADISE OF GOD:

AND I DEDICATE IT TO MY SPIRITUAL FATHERS,

ST. CHARLES

AND

ST. FRANCIS OF ASSISL

CONTENTS.

PROLOGUE.

THE Evening Star shone, like a Topaz, in the sky : and the gray twilight began to creep over the world. A great river was flowing without a ripple to the sea. The trees on its banks dipped their branches in it as it passed, but did not ruffle its glassy stream. The sea lay peacefully out-spread at the foot of the valley through which that river took its way. The leafy boughs waved noiselessly in the air. The gloaming lay upon the land and sea.

The darkness deepened on the world : and the wind rustled in the branches.

The bats wheeled through the air; the snails came out; and the hooting of the owls was heard. The stream was quickly blown into deep ripples and the boughs of the trees sank in it heavily as it passed. It rushed onward to the sea. Far away countless flakes of foam began to gleam through the darkness upon the

crests of the waves. Then was heard the low
muttering of the storm.

Swiftly the storm rose in its strength: it
swept over land and sea: the midnight lay
upon the world. 'The great trees swayed back-
ward and forward wildly in the arms of the
wind. Deeply they plunged their branches in
the stream as it passed; as it sped onward
through the valley to the stormy sea. The
thunder rolled upon the mountains, and the
lightning with its forked flashes lit up the
murkiness of the night. The waves looked as
if they were churned, and dashed against the
rocks in a sheet of foam. Every moment
the fierce gale swept onward with new strength,
flinging the white-crested water against the
crags. In the mist the spray was driven far over
the fields.

A ship with bare spars came drifting through
the darkness. Breakers were foaming round
her like a sea of milk. Helpless before the
rage of the storm she drifted onward to the
rocks. Dark and over-hanging, those rocks
stood up in the white sea. They are dreadful as
they pierce the starless night. The sea is
hungry ; and the ravenous waves are crying out

for their food. The wind is rushing on wildly, as if it were shrieking with pain.

The crags, hard and cold, stand up in their strength amid the breakers and the pealing of the thunder.

The ship drifts on through the water and the darkness; and a wild wailing rises above the voice of the storm. Again and again, the flashes of the lightning cast a fitful gleam on the white sea, on the rocks, on the great ship drifting swiftly to her doom. Again and again the wailing rises above the shrieks of the wind, and above the thud of the angry waves.

The cliffs, wet and slippery, stand up from the gleaming breakers as they spread themselves out with a seething sound, all boiling in foam round the craggy heights. The ship drifts on through the midnight, through the roaring waves, through the lightning's gleam.

The darkness grows murkier ; the wind is stronger ; the sea is fiercer. The flashes of the forked lightning are brighter and more startling in the blackness of the gloom.

With a fearful crash the ship drives against the rocks ; is splintered ; and begins to sink. As it sinks it is rifted by the lightning. The

cry of a great anguish rises above the howling
of the wind. The waves rush on. Then, after
a while, a shriek, long and piercing, struck the
face of the astonished night. The hard pillars
of rock tingled with it as it passed. Those
slippery crags gave no hold to the fingers of
the drowning. The waves are shouting over
their prey.

After that piercing shriek there was no cry
but the shrill cry of the seagulls, startled in the
darkness, and driven headlong before the storm.

The wind lifted the breakers; lifted them up
and hurled them against the cliffs. The dun
foam was blown far over the land. Through
the midnight came the uproar of the storm, and
the dash of the restless waves. The beetling
rocks stood up in their anger. No ship, no
swimmers, were to be seen. The terns and
the cormorants flew screaming over the sea.
The wind drove the breakers onward.

HOMEWARD.

CHAPTER I.

IN THE DARK.

A BRIDE of the crucified King wandered from the light into the darkness. The Crown fell from her head, and His Face was hidden. She who had been sitting in morning-brightness now dwelt in the shadow of the night. No longer did she walk among the Lilies in the King's Garden, but dimly through the gloom she could see the Plumes of Death. Ashes were on her head instead of a Crown; and she wore sackcloth instead of the white raiment of her Espousals. From the sunshine and the sparkling river, from the flowers and the fruitful trees, from all the gladness of her Home, she had passed forth in her desolation and sorrow

to the land where demons and monsters meet.
The thistle grows in its fortresses, and thorns
and nettles in its houses. The raven dwells
there, and there the kites are gathered together.
There beneath the midnight she sat in the dens
of dragons, in the dwellings of worms and bats
and creeping things. She was bitten by
serpents, and their poisoned fangs had touched
her heart. There was one wound in the heart
from which none ever recovered, but she was
not bitten in that way, for she had not yet come
to the time when that bite could be given.
Weeping bitter tears in her loneliness and woe
she tried to think of the Home from which she
had wandered, and of the Home, more blessed
and more glorious still, among the Lilies of
the New Creation. Then a nameless anguish
rested on her soul, as the remembrance of the
promised land rose up before her; as she thought
of that lost blessedness which was the way to
the Paradise of God.

Thus, far away from the light, in her darkness
and sorrow, she heard the rushing of the Storm ;
and the sound of its wailing pierced her heart
with anguish, when she thought of the voice of
the King. But a light of love was still burning

in her Home. Though she could not see them,
yet she knew of the Watchfires, burning by day
and night. Their flames, like pillars of fire,
were always rising through the mists; but she
could not see them because of the darkness that
hung before her eyes. A great agony filled her
heart; and for a moment she knew not whether
any way might still lie open to the once-pro-
mised Home. Then through the gloom the
voice of the King sounded in her ears, and the
pity of the King overshadowed her, and the
love of the King filled her heart. For a moment
there was blackness without a star, a midnight
to which morning might never come. Then
came the glimmering of the Day. Infinite
tenderness, infinite compassion, encircled the
Wanderer. An everlasting love was round her
lonely anguish: and a gleam of the morning-
brightness shone through the clouds of the
night. A ray of hope fell on the poor Wanderer,
as she sat uncrowned, far away from her Home,
in the shadow of the sable Plumes. The dark
River flowed past her as she wept in her sorrow;
flowed swiftly and fiercely past her through the
Desert to the Sea. Its waters kept rising round
her: they came nearer and nearer, and every

moment she thought that they would sweep her
away. She could just see them through the
night : and that made it all more fearful, as she
said with trembling, 'These pitiless waters will
sweep me away through the darkness; these
wild waters will bear me away lifeless to the Sea.'

Thus, in the Dark, she bowed her head in the
dimness of pain. Her anguish was fearful to
see. The devouring River swept past her,
and its rushing sounded like the doom in her
ears. She said, 'These waters will carry me
away for ever.' She was on the brink of the
dark River, far away from the morning brightness, in bitterness of soul. Amid the gloom a
crushing weight lay on her heart, as she heard the
storm and thought of the Home from which she
had wandered. The sable Plumes were drooping sorrowfully, as she sat amid her tears, trying
to see the Watchfires on the Jasper Towers. The
River swept on, fiercely and darkly, to the Sea.

Then it seemed as if the King were standing
beside her ; and His Divine Presence heartened
her, and gave her hope. So she said to Him,
in a sorrowful voice ; ' Through this darkness I
stretch out my hands to Thee, Divine Love,
from Whom I have fallen. I cry out to Thee in

my broken-hearted misery. I lift up my hands
to Thee and beseech Thee to help me.' She
heard the voice of the King in a moment, assur-
ing her of His pity and His love.

He said, 'I will not leave thee; I will not
forsake thee.' But she could scarcely believe
such blessed words, and she answered; 'But
my sins, Divine Love, are so many that I cannot
number them : they are more than the hairs of
my head: my heart hath failed me. They
have taken such hold upon me that I cannot
look up. I mourn over them in the bitterness
of my soul. They stand before me in this
darkness and frighten me and make me tremble.
Wilt Thou not cast me away for ever? Shall I
ever again see Thy Face? Wilt Thou ever
restore to me Thy Holy Spirit? O forsake me
not utterly, Thou God of my salvation.' Then
a second time she heard Him saying to her, 'I
will not leave thee; I will not forsake thee.'
Still she could not take comfort from His words,
but said, 'I hear Thy Voice, Divine Love, and
am not comforted. Thou hast stricken me, and
I am afflicted. I have mingled ashes with my
drink and my bread has been wet with tears. I
have made myself drunk with wormwood and

gall. O that my eyes could have seen Thee,
and that I had known Thee for what Thou art.
I knew not what I was doing when I went out
into the darkness and storm. I knew not,
Divine Love, what I was doing when I went to
the worms and creeping things. Yet I did know,
but it was only darkly. Still I knew enough to
hinder me from doing as I did. Now a great
sorrow fills my soul in this darkness, and the
storm beats so fiercely on me that I can not look
up. I went out from my Home : I went out
from Thee : and now I am lost in misery, and
now my wretchedness hides me. O Divine
Love, in this night-season, I am crying to Thee.
I am sick with sorrow and dread ; and to whom
can I go but to Thee ?' Then a third time,
through the darkness, came to her the comforting words; 'I will not leave thee : I will
not forsake thee.'

All this time, you must remember, she was
frightened by the rushing of the River, and by
the waving of the sable Plumes. So she did
not understand these words as she ought to have
understood them : but, even while the King
was speaking to her, wept bitterly. Uncrowned,
in her desolate sorrow, she cowered beneath the

Plumes of Death. In sackcloth and ashes she sat trembling by the fierce River. Through the darkness dimly she saw the mighty stream go by. She said ' These cold waters will carry me away lifeless to the Sea.' Yet this voice of love came to her through the Tempest; and a glimmer of light shone on her through the gloom. Her utter hopelessness passed away. But still a great fear sat throned in her heart. She thought of the Home that she had lost, and the very thought was anguish. She thought also of the love that would have been hers : and a nameless pain overwhelmed her. Silently she wrung her hands. Unconsciously she gazed into the darkness. She forgot the River rushing onward: and did not hear the anger of the Storm. She thought only of the joy that would have been hers in the beauty of her Home. For a moment the sable Plumes seemed to be the Lilies and Pomegranates by the Crystal River. Then her sorrow came over her like a flood. She clasped her hands on her knees, and bowed her head upon them in speechless anguish. Only the sound of a low moaning went forth to the dews of the night.

In agony of soul she bowed her head upon her hands.

To this hour I feel the iron that entered into my own soul when I saw the greatness and bitterness of her grief.

The storm-wind rushed past on its mighty wings : and the River swept onward to the Sea.

CHAPTER II.

THROUGH THE TORRENT.

THE King came from the light into the darkness, seeking for His Bride. With a deathless love in His Heart He left His Home to seek and to save that which was lost. He took His Crown from His Head, and laid aside His Sceptre, and put off His royal Apparel. Then He clothed Himself with poor raiment, and with His Staff in His Hand, in the dead of the night, went out of the Door of His Palace, closing it after Him till the time of His return. His friends knew not His thoughts and did not understand His ways.

When He went out into the night, His Eyes were full of tears, because of the greatness of His pity and His love. Thus He was drawn to His Bride in her sackcloth and ashes. There was no anger in His Heart as He went, but only His love and His unfathomable pity. A great sorrow overshadowed Him, as He took

His way through the night. A strong Wind
swept up against Him from the Desert, and the
pitiless Rain was driven in His Face. Sharp
Flints cut His Feet : and the Thorns and Briers
tore His Hands. His way was wet with tears
and blood. His lost Bride lifted up her hands
to Him in the anguish of her soul : sorrowfully
and pleadingly called out to Him lest He should
pass her in the Dark. The sable Plumes were
waving in the Wind ; and I saw that one touched
her cheek, as she said, ' Come to me, my Saviour,
in this unutterable agony.' The Rain beat upon
Him as He went, and the Wind swept up from
the Desert.

But He had never been more beautiful than
then. The look of anguish on His Face made
Him more worshipful than ever. Now His
Princes saw a look in His Face which they had
never seen before. Even in the dark they saw
it, for the light of His own Beauty was round
Him and on His way. He had been altogether
lovely in His Kingdom, but now in new beauty
He enters the sanctuary of their hearts. Weary
and footsore, hungry and thirsty, full of love
and full of sorrow, He passed on through the
Storm, through the blinding Rain, through the

Wind that swept up from the Desert and the Sea.
He came to the Torrent through which He
had to pass that He might bring back the
Wanderer. There was no anger in His Heart
as He went down into its-depths; but only, as I
said, His love and His measureless pity. The
torrent flowed fiercely; its waters were red;
and the Wind lifted it in crimson waves. She
for whom He was seeking sat beyond it, desolate
in her sorrow. Lonely with a great loneliness
she waited for His coming. Her clasped hands
were reaching out to Him in an agony of
mingled hope and fear, and her voice, still sweet
in His Ears, was borne to Him over the waters
of the Flood. Pleadingly she lifted up her hands
to Him through the midnight : stretched forth
her clasped hands to Him through the darkness
and the storm. She called to Him across the
waters of the Flood, and said 'Come to me my
Love, for I am lost and helpless.'

He came and looked at the Torrent. His
Divine Sorrow lighted up the darkness. He
folded His Hands in prayer, and looked stead-
fastly through the night to the Home that He
had left. It seemed as if, for a moment, He
were thinking whether there could be found any

other way of reaching the Wanderer beyond the
Flood. But it only seemed to be so. As I
looked, He went forward, calmly, with fearless
steps.

He went down into the Torrent. The waters
covered His Feet; they came up to His Knees;
they reached His Heart; they swept fiercely
over His Head. He went down into the deep
waters, and they closed over Him, and swallowed
Him up. But His love burned more brightly in
the depths of those many waters, shining like a
star through the Flood and through the night.
That love, deathless and changeless, bore Him
up through the red waves; till, like the brightness of the morning, He stood upon the Shore.

He came to His lost Bride: and the flood of
His tenderness filled her soul. He stooped
down, rejoicing over her. He was silent over her
in His love. Then in great gladness the
Wanderer lay forgiven, in His Arms, and on His
Heart.

Just as the King was passing through the
Torrent, His Bride, not knowing how near He
was, called out to Him in her misery and
said; 'I am crying out to Thee, Divine Love,
and Thou dost not hear me. My voice can not

pierce through these waterfloods, through the
rushing of this stream. I am away from Thee,
and Thou canst not hear me. In vain, in vain, I
lift up my prayer to Thee.' Then a very gentle
voice, exceedingly sweet, fell on her ears, above
all the fury of the Storm, and it came to her
thus ; 'I do hear thee and I am coming to save
thee. I will bring thee from the place in which
thou hast lost thyself in the dark and the cloudy
day.'

But the lost Bride of the King could scarcely
believe that she heard rightly, when she heard
such words as these. She said to Him; 'Divine
Lover of my soul, do I hear rightly ? Do I
understand what Thou sayest ? Wilt Thou
save me ? Canst Thou seek for me and love me
after all that I have done ? ' Never to this hour
has there faded from her mind the memory of
what she felt, when she heard the answer of the
King. Never, to all eternity, can that remembrance have one shadow of dimness upon it.
He said ; 'I have loved thee with an everlasting
love ; and therefore with loving-kindness I will
draw thee to Myself, taking pity on thee.' This
answer is as fresh in her heart now as it was
when the promise was fulfilled. She knew not

what she answered in her joy : 'Then I am not
lost ; my Love, Thou hast not forsaken me ; I am
still Thine; Thy Own Bride, loved and lost
and found again, and loved still more.'

But the King heaped up gladness on gladness, and love on love. He said to her ; ' I will
put away all thy transgressions and all thy sins :
as far as the East is from the West, so far they
shall be put away from thee. Though they be
as crimson and scarlet they shall be as wool and
snow.'

All this time He was drawing nearer ; the
Storm kept on getting fiercer ; and the waves
were far bigger and far stronger than before.
But His suffering only drew her soul to Him
more and more, as she said ; ' All my heart
turns to Thee, Thou merciful Spouse. Now,
with a great hope and a great love, through my
misery I lift up my hands to Thee. Do not
tarry, Divine love ; come to me quickly, and
do not leave me in this darkness; do not leave
me, Thou compassionate Saviour, in this prison
of death. My whole soul is bowed down at the
sight of Thy woe: and I tremble when I think
of the strength of this Torrent.'

Nearer He came in His Divine loveliness ;

nearer He came in the greatness of His strength. The waves were rising higher, as He spoke this promise ; ' I will make a way through the great deep, and I will carry thee through the flood.'

Then it seemed to me as if He lifted His Bride in His Arms, that just before had been stretched out like a cross; and I heard her saying ; ' How strong these waves are, and how dreadful is this River. But, my Love, Thou art stronger; with Thee I cannot fear ; Thy everlasting Arms are safely round me, and I lie on Thy Sacred Heart, as the great Torrent rushes by. I was afraid of the thunder and the lightning, but I am not afraid now. But what is this, my Crucified Love ? What are these tears in Thy Eyes ? What are these streams of blood on Thy Face ? A moment ago I saw Thee beautiful and glorious, now I see Thee stricken and disfigured : and yet, Divine Love, Thou never didst seem to me so beautiful as now. What are these Tears ? What is this Anguish ? ' It pierced her to the heart, when she knew that she could not help Him, and when these words fell on her ears; ' With a great price I must purchase for thee thy freedom ; through a great agony

I must save thee.' Still she could not help
saying to Him; 'Can I do nothing to help
Thee? Can I do nothing to console Thee,
Divine and beautiful Love?' Then He said;
'Thou canst not help Me, for I must tread
the Wine-press alone. But thou canst console
Me : thy love is My consolation.'

Thus He answered her as the great River
swept onward to the Sea ; and thus she spoke
to Him and gazed in His Face, as He carried
her through the Torrent. The devouring
waters threatened to bear Him away : but His
Staff held Him up in the midst of the Flood
and His ransomed Bride lay safely on His
Heart. She felt strong in her helplessness for
He was strong ; and now it was her gladness
that He was saving her when she could not
save herself. It was her joy to have nothing
of her own, to owe everything to Him, and
to know that without Him she could do nothing. The strong Wind swept over Him;
, the Rain was driven in His Face ; the overflowing water passed by. Safely above those
angry waters He lifted up His Bride. Victor-
iously He held her above them as they rushed
swiftly to the Sea. He carried His Staff with

Him. Sometimes it seemed as if the Waves would cover Him for ever. Then with one pierced Hand He held His Staff, and it stayed Him up against the rushing Waters : and with the other He bore His Bride safely above the foaming Stream. All the while there was in His Heart an inexhaustible love; all the while there was in His Eyes an unfathomable pity.

His Warriors with their glittering Spears looked on with wonder and awe. They rejoiced in the greatness of their strength, for He had made them strong ; but a strength like this strength of the King they had never known. They stood in two long lines of brightness, like streams of burning gold, and the King passed on between them. They had seen Him and had knelt before Him in His Home : and there the beauty of His Face had filled and overflowed their hearts with love and gladness. Now they see Him in weakness and suffering, and yet He looks as beautiful as ever. Their hearts are filled with wonder and love as they gaze upon His pain-stricken Face. Yet they think that It never looked more beautiful than now. Its beauty even seems to grow with its sorrow. Lovingly and conqueringly He carried His

B

Bride through the midst of the Army of His
Warriors : and with great reverence they bowed
their golden Helmets as He passed.

It did indeed fill my heart with gladness to
see how love and holy fear were mingled in the
faces of those majestic Princes.

Never had there been a love like this love of
the King. The great Waters could not quench
it : and the Floods could not drown it. He
shone in strength and brightness through the
blackness of the Storm. He rose in His peerless
beauty over the waters of the Flood. Above
those dark Waves He lifted up His Hands. He
bore His Bride through the Torrent : He carried
her on His Heart. He was red in His Apparel
and His Garments were dyed in blood. Her
Cloak and Veil were stained with the crimson
Stream. Very trustfully, very reverently, very
lovingly, she gazed on His Face. The Storm
beat upon Him, and the Rain was driven in His
Eyes. The mighty Torrent rushed by ; and
drove onward in its headlong course. His Staff
again and again bore Him up in its rushing
waters. The Wind swept against Him from the
Desert and shook Him as it passed. With a
great love and a great pity in His Soul, with a

great light on His sorrowful Face, He carried His Bride in His Arms, on His Heart, through the wind-shaken Waters, through the crimson Waves, through the great River sweeping onward past the Desert to the Sea.

CHAPTER III.

THUS He passed through the Torrent; and thus He carried His redeemed Spouse through the Flood. With a fierce stream the dark River came down from the Mountains: with a fierce stream the red River plunged onward to the Sea. The Rain was driven in His Face as He came, and the Wind from the Desert swept over the Water and shook Him with its blasts. Wild wailings, shrieks of pain and fear, came up on the wings of that strong Wind as it drove onward over the Stream.

Tenderly and graciously the King bore His Bride through the River. Lovingly and fearlessly she lay upon His Heart, gazing on His Face through the rain. The lightning lighted up the sky, and the thunder shook the hills; but no fear came near her: she only lay more reverently in His Divine Arms. Sometimes it seemed, as I said before, as if He must be swept away by the Torrent rushing down from the

Mountains; but no fear came near her; she only lay more trustingly, more reverently, on His Divine Heart.

His Staff held Him up amid the Water. The dark Stream swept by. Patiently and fearlessly, feeling His way step by step, He bore her through the River. The black Stream swept by. With great gladness He came to the bank and stood clear of the Water. The red Stream swept on, past the Desert to the Sea.

A light of triumph shone in the faces of His Princes, as they stood round Him on the bank, and sang their Hymn of praise for the greatness of His victory. As they stood singing before Him, their voices pierced the clouds, far above the rushing of the Stream. So sweet, so strong, was the voice of that Hymn that no one heard the noise of the River sweeping down fiercely from the Hills. There was always great joy among the Princes when a Wanderer was brought back from beneath the sable Plumes.

So on the bank of the River the King stood with His Bride in the midst of His Warriors. Her Hood and her Cloak were now as I saw of silver-gray; but a Veil still covered her.

She had an Olive-branch in her hand.

The Desert lay before her ; and there was a Road, long and weary, stretching across it and leading to her Home.

She had to go along the Road by herself. When the King brought her to the Bank He told her this. Very gently He told her, and she did not shrink back from the truth, because she heard it from Him. If another had told her she could not have borne it. He knew this and told her Himself. With such Divine gentleness He told her, that the truth, coming to her from His Lips, seemed to be a blessing. She remembered how those Lips, just before, had been parched up and burnt with the great agony that filled His Heart, when He said, ' I thirst.'

So she had to go along the Road by herself, for she would be unable to see Him, but He promised always to be near her. His being away from her in the weary journey was a sorrow that she had brought on herself : but His Presence, hidden and veiled, was the gift of His love. Her heart fainted within her when she looked at the glittering sands and the long Road leading through them to her Home. But He heartened her by His Words. Her soul seemed to faint with fear ; but, in His Divine Compassion, He drew her to Himself, and for a moment she felt the touch of His Hand. She looked and He was gone : then, strengthened and comforted, she went forward on her way. She could hear the flowing of the River ; and there came to her an echo of the Wind that swept up from the Desert and the Sea. There also came to her a sound as of a distant Battle. But that sound was so faint that she could scarcely hear it.

Now the King in His mercy did not leave her to go along that Road unrefreshed, on her Homeward way. When He went out of the Door of His Home He had great love and great pity in His Heart. If it could be, He was now more loving, more pitiful, than ever. His Bride rejoiced in this. His pity was dearer to her than all things else but His love. So He did not leave her to the merciless sands. Here and there, as it seemed good to Him, He had planted Palm Trees in the Desert ; and had made Fountains of Water.

For a moment she stood beside Him. Then He went away, and she set off on her journey. She wore, as I told you just now, a gray Hood

and Cloak reaching down to her bare feet ; and
a dark Veil covered her. Her Olive-branch was
in her hand.

Very hopeful because of His words and His
love, she faced the sands of the Desert. The
sun beat on her head, and the sand blistered her
feet. She was always kneeling down and
stretching out her clasped hands to the King,
though she could not see Him ; but not now in
lonely sorrow. She remembered the rushing of
the Torrent, and the Rain that had been driven
in His Face.

Day after day she kept on her way : time
after time the King met her in the places of
refreshment, by the Wells in the Desert.
Under the Palm Trees He met her ; and by the
Fountains of Water He gave her drink.

The way was often harder than she thought
that it would be. Sometimes she felt as if
for very weariness she must lie down and die;
and sometimes she felt as if her heart would
break, not only with its grief but with its love.
But whenever her heart fainted most, and whenever her strength failed most, she came to the
Palm Trees and the murmuring Fountain.
Always under the Palms the King came to her,

and strengthened her, and gave her rest. They were to her a cloud by day, and a place of refuge, and a covert from the whirlwind and the storm.

The thought of these meetings strengthened her on her road. Oftentimes her heart seemed to die within her : and then she used to say to herself, ' It is only a little while, though it seems a long while, since I have been with Him. It is only a little while, though it seems a long while, before I shall be with Him again.' Then she was heartened and went on. She remembered the look on His Face when the Rain was driven into it and the strong Wind swept over Him : and she was heartened and went on. The love of the King filled her soul, and she did not faint by the way. She always, though darkly and as through a glass, could see the Face that had been spit upon for her. Through the love of the King, she came ever to a Fountain of Water when she was parched up with thirst : but in His fearful thirst no Water had touched His burnt-up Lips.

Thus under the Palms He always met her, and there she rested in His love. The sands of the Desert lay round that resting-place, and the rays of the sun beat fiercely on it: but the fan-like leaves of the Palm Trees spread themselves out against the sky; and the Stream flowed downward from the Fountain. The birds sang overhead, as she sat with the King under the shadow of the Trees. There she drank of the chalice of His love. His chosen Warriors, in their resplendent beauty, stood round the Fountain with their Swords and glittering Spears.

When the time came for her to go, He always laid His pierced Hands on her head very lovingly, and blessed her. So in great gladness she gazed on His beautiful Face, as yet only dimly seen : and all His love fell upon her, as the Palms waved their branches. His Princes always longed to understand these things, and were filled with joy.

As she went from one resting-place to another, I heard her praying thus ; ' Help me, Divine Love, among these sands, or I must lie down and die. The heat and the long way make me so tired, that I can scarcely drag myself along. Help me, Divine Love, in this Wilderness or I must perish. Help me, Incarnate Love, among these sands or I must lie down and die.'

At once there came to her an answer like

this : 'I am with thee, thou redeemed one, though thou seest Me not ; I am beside thee in this Desert. Did I bring thee through the Torrent to leave thee here? Did I save thee, when the Rain was driven in My Face and the Wind swept over Me from the Sea, that after all I should let thee die beneath the burning sun?

Then she seemed to be smitten with self-reproach for her faithlessness, and said ; O my Crucified Love, forgive me my distrust, for I am weak and sinful. It is not distrust, dear Lord, as Thou knowest, though it seems to be so. But I am not as Thou art. Thou canst walk in Thy Own strength, but I cannot take one step without Thee. I cry out to Thee and say, ' Why dost Thou forsake me?' I cry out in my weakness and fear, but I do not mean what I say. Thou knowest that I do not mean it : but in my sorrow I cannot help crying out thus to Thee. Thou knowest that I would not say it to any one else. Divine Love, I am full of fear. Shall I never come to the Palm Trees? Shall I never reach the Fountain of Water? O my Love, Thou art merciful : help me in this wilderness or I must die.'

' Remember the Darkness from which I

brought thec,' answered the King, ' and the Torrent through which I carried thee. Remember
the words that I spake to thee, and the love
with which I loved thee, and the rest that I
gave to thee on My Heart: then thou shalt
know that at the time most wisely chosen I
will be with thee. When most thou needest Me
thou shalt come to Me; and the Palm Trees
shall wave over thee, and thou shalt hear the
murmuring of the Water.' These words
strengthened her, and enabled her to go on.
In a little while she passed, by the goodness of
the King, to one of the Islands of green. Then
I heard her say; 'O my Love, I am with Thee
now, beneath the Palms and beside this
Fountain, in Thy wealthy rest. The sun does
not scorch me now: the sands do not
burn me now: the Desert does not frighten
me now. I see the glare of the sand
through these leaves of the underwood, but it
only makes this Home of rest more precious.
To me, dear Lord, Thou art all in all. I know
that I must go forth again beneath the sun, but
I cannot fear it now, for I cannot think of it
now. I can think only of Thee. It will be
time enough for me to think of my dreary way

when I must go. Now, Divine Love, I am a seal on Thy Arm, and a seal on Thy Heart.'

Thus, from time to time, she rested under the Palms. Then strengthened and comforted by the love of the King she faced the sands of the Desert, and went Homeward according to His Will. The shadow of those Trees lay upon her soul, and the sound of the Water murmured in her heart, as she went onward. The sun beat fiercely on her, and the end seemed very far off; but she went onward to her Home. The King waited for her always under the Palms, on her way. There she lay hidden from suffering in the shelter of His Sacred Heart. The Trees made a shade in the Desert, and kept off the heat of the sun. Thus she ever found rest in her weariness. Had it not been for this she would have died on the way. But, when the sun was hottest, then she came to the shelter of the Palms, and rested with her Divine Love. If all the words in the world were put together they could not shadow forth the blessedness of that rest. The branches of the Trees waved gently over her; and the Water sounded in her ears. Then with new strength she took her way again through the Desert.

She drew her Hood well over her face and gathered her Cloak closely round her as she went barefooted over the sands. Her long Veil covered her. Again and again through the distance there came to her the sound of the River and the Wind. Again and again there came also to her a faint echo of the Battle.

Round her, though she saw them not, there were the armed Warriors of the King: and away over the sand there gleamed lines of silver Spears.

Her Olive-branch in her hand was fresh and green. So she went Homeward through the sands of the Desert. From time to time, as she went, the waving Palm Trees were a shade from the heat, and from the brightness of the rays that the sun poured down upon the thirsty sand.

CHAPTER IV.

SHE passed onward over the sand-ridges, onward through the Desert, onward beneath the sun. Sometimes fainting by the way, she passed onward to her Home. The thought of that Home upheld her : for she knew of the love waiting for her within its doors ; of the Watch-fires burning by day and night. Always lonely, save beneath the shadow of the Palms, and sometimes almost hopeless amid the landwaves of sand, she went onward to the Eastern Mountains and the glimmering Dawn that came over their Cedar-crown.

The Home to which she was now going was built on the highest of those Mountains; and on all of them the Cedars were ever growing.

Through morning, noon, and afternoon, she hastened on her way, resting from time to time by the Fountains of Water. She went quickly

along the road leading to her Home, and turned
not aside and tarried not. A Divine Love was
waiting for her in that Home of Light, and so
she hastened on her way. Ever as she went she
remembered the Torrent through which the
King had carried her, and the Rain that was
driven in His face : and again and again she
seemed to catch an echo of the Wind that swept
up from the Desert and the Sea. The sun fell
fiercely on her head ; but she walked quickly
Homeward.

She passed beneath the Evening Star. The
sun went down behind the waves of sand.
Sometimes he went down, through the mist,
like a red shield of fire, and sometimes he set
amid violet clouds. The cool breezes came up
from the outskirts of the Desert. The moon
sat beneath the purple canopy of her throne,
and the stars thronged round her in the sky.
The breath of a gentle wind stirred the Palm
Trees. Throbbing and gleaming above the
Bride hung the myriad-starred Heaven ; and all
around her was the pitiless sand.

She heard the song of the stars above her
head and the voice of praise that rose from the
silvery moon. The night was dark to the

brightness of the day: but it was light to the darkness of that gloom from which she had been brought. Whenever the Evening Star came up with her radiant sisters, the Bride thought of the darkness through which she had lifted up her hands; through which she had stretched forth her clasped hands, pleadingly, to the King. Then the night drew round her its sheltering veil, and she lay down to rest. But, while she slept, her heart was waking, was always turning to her Home. She dreamed of the Fountain and the Palm Trees. The rustling branches made ever a melody round her; and the voice of the water was music in her heart. But far sweeter was the remembrance which she had of the Voice of the King. Even in sleep she had that remembrance, as her waking heart turned to Him.

So she rested; and His love overshadowed her, and the perils of the night did not make her afraid.

Sometimes indeed beneath the stars, in the coolness of the night, she would go a little way on her road: but not often, not far. Her Love had given her the day for walking, and the night for sleep. As she slept He watched over

C

her. The darkness was not darkness to Him, and the night was as clear as the day. He had gone to her when she sat in sackcloth and ashes beneath the Plumes of Death. He saw her anguish of soul, and loved her and pitied her and brought her from the iron prison. He had lifted her in His strong Arms, as the devouring Torrent swept by. Again and again, under the scorching sun, He came to her in the islands of rest. Beneath the stars, as she slept, He watched over her; and the darkness to Him was light.

As He watched He could hear, in the stillness of the night, the rushing of the River, and the Wind that had driven up the Rain.

Then it seemed as if in her sleep she spoke to Him, and heard His Voice. She said, 'I sleep, Divine Love, but my heart waketh: Thou art standing beside me. In Thy love and Thy pity Thou overshadowest me; in the darkness Thou art my light.' 'I remember the time,' the King answered, 'when I slept for thee in death upon the Cross. Then there came to Me the night in which no man can work. Then was My Heart broken with love.' 'O, crucified Love,' she said, 'I too remember that time;

and it comes to me even in my dreams. How could I forget it? Is there not a love stronger than death? Is not Thy love for me stronger than the dark River? That love comes to me in this sleep, the sister of death. Now, Divine Love, my heart waketh to Thee.' Then I saw the Princes moving about, and though it was dark round the sleeper the light fell on their glittering Spears. The King said : 'I give sleep to My beloved that they may rest and be refreshed after the burden and heat of the day.'

Words like these always lighted up the faces of the Warriors. They listened as she answered : 'I know it, my Lord and my God. What have I that Thou dost not give? To whom else can I go? To whom else can I turn? Thou hast the words of eternal life. I am shrivelled up in the loveless world, but my heart opens out to Thee, as the flowers open out to the sun. My soul is as a leaf burnt up by the heat; but the dew of Thy love refreshes me. Even through the darkness Thy light is shining on me; for with Thee there is no night; and the darkness and the light are both alike to Thee.'

As I listened I heard this; 'My Eyes are looking on thee; My Ears are open to thee.

I keep thee as safely from the pestilence and the terror of the night, as from the arrow that flieth by noon-day.'

These words made her say even in sleep ; ' O, pitiful Love, I lie down in peace, and take my rest, for Thou and Thou only keepest me safely beneath these stars and these swiftly-flying clouds.'

When I looked up, the clouds were driving across the sky. Sometimes they hid one star and sometimes another: and sometimes they hung like fleecy veils before the moon. The moon never looked so beautiful as when half-hidden in cloud.

One thing I remember well. The night was very clear, and the stars were very bright. Suddenly a great gleam fell on the sand. The points of all the silver Spears glittered so that they were just like the stars that were hanging above us in the sky.

Thus in the Desert she rested beneath the Evening Star. The King stood beside her, as she slept. Among the dew and the drops of the night He looked through the lattices. There He waited till the passing away of the shadows and the breaking of the day. His Divine Face was near her, and she saw it through her sleep. She knew that He was there, and even through sleep she turned to that Heart that ever loved her with such a deathless love as the tyranny was passing away. That Divine Heart was filled with love and pity. So she slept in safety ; and the perils of the night did not make her afraid. Thus it was that the King gave sleep to His beloved.

His Princes gathered round Him, as He watched over the Bride, resting on her Homeward way. By His light they saw her Hood and Cloak of silver-gray through her Veil. Like gleams of dawn they came through the darkness ; like flashes of light they passed over the Desert. They remembered the time when their King put off His royal apparel and clothed Himself in poor raiment and took His Staff and stepped out of the door of His Home and went on into the night. Then they did not understand what He was doing ; but they loved and adored Him, knowing His might and wisdom. Now they begin to see the mysteries into which then they wished to look. All through the night, like glimmerings of day, they gather round Him, and gaze with a

great love on His Bride. You would have rejoiced to see how reverently those armed Warriors of the King watched over her, as she slept with a waking heart beneath the stars. Their Swords were on their thighs and their Spears in their hands, because of fears in the night. One of these Princes never left her, for the King had told him to stay always at her side. He had been with her even beyond the River, among the ashes. He ever gave her great help as she went on her way.

The fresh air came up from the outskirts of the Desert; the stars hung overhead in the brightness of their shining; and the moon sat beneath the purple canopy of her throne. The pillars of her throne were like silver. In the Desert the King watched with a great love over her whom He had carried through the Torrent, when the Rain was driven in His Face. He stood among His Warriors, bright and strong, but He Himself was far stronger, far brighter, than all. Even in the darkness you could see the gleaming of their Helmets and their silver Spears. Sweet sleep rested upon her in the midst of those shining Legions, but through their brightness and through the gloom of the night her heart was always turning to the King who had Himself come from the darkness of the grave.

Night by night He watched over her, when the stars came out; and night by night He caught an echo of the Wind that swept up, in the old days, from the Desert.

So, with fresh heart, she rose up in the morning-light; and took her Homeward way through the sand towards the Dawn, ever brightening over the Eastern Mountains with their Cedar-crown.

CHAPTER V.

THE Bride of the King thus rested among his Princes. With a great love He watched over her, and through her sleep she was ever turning with her whole heart to Him. His Warriors stood round her in the darkness beneath the stars. Their Swords, as I told you, were on their thighs, because of fears in the night.

Through the silence they heard faintly the Wind that swept up with the Rain, and the River that was ever rushing to the Sea.

Then morning came ; and the stars hid themselves from the sun. The Bride rose up, and went on her way. Again she went towards her Home through the thirsty sands : and oftentimes, faint and weary, wished for the end.

On her road the King waited for her, as you know, under the Palm Trees ; but there were long Desert-spaces, where she sought Him and found Him not. So she would have died by

the way, if the sure love of the King had not
been to her a Shadow in the day-time from
the heat. She could not always reach the
shelter of the Palms, but she could always find
Him in her own heart. She could turn ever
to the thought of His love. She could talk to
herself about Him, and call to mind the things
that He had done, and the promises that He
had made : and this thought of the King, of
His love for her, of her love for Him, was
to her as the Shadow of a great Rock.

The sun beat fiercely on her, as she went
Homeward. She often longed for the Fountains
of Water, but always for strength she turned to
the Divine love in her own soul: and thus the
Sacred Heart of the King was to her a shelter
in the Desert. Rivers of Water thus flowed
for her in the sands, and the Shadow of a great
Rock saved her from the burning heat.

It was not of course exactly the same thing
as the coming of the King under the Palm
Trees. There He was actually present. There
He was with her as truly as He was with His
Princes, but they could see Him and she could
see Him not; save only, as I said before,
darkly and as it were through a glass. But, as

the shade of the Rock, He was in her heart :
and thus it depended on her love, whether He
were a shade to her from the heat, or not. The
more that she loved Him and thought of
Him, the more He dwelt with her : but if ever
her love began to grow cold then the sun grew
hotter. So when she loved Him very deeply
the Shadow was very refreshing. Still at the
best, you see, it was not the same thing as the
Presence of the King by the Fountain of Waters.

On her way, she talked thus to herself: 'I
cannot speak of the beauty of the King nor of
the pricelessness of His love : I cannot speak of
them, for I cannot think of them. They are
far beyond me in their height and depth. The
more that I think of His love, the less I seem
able to understand it. One day I shall know
clearly what He is, what His love is, but now I
do not. Yet I do know that there is no beauty,
no strength, no love, like His. With unchanging
gladness I know that He loves me and will love
me for ever. But for this knowledge I should
die. I should fall here in the sand if it were not
for His love. To me that love is the Shadow
of a great Rock. I remember the look that
was on His face when He found me in my

sackcloth ; and how with a great pity and a great tenderness He bent over me and wiped the tears from my cheeks with His pierced Hand. I remember too how he bore me through the Torrent, when the Rain was driven in His Face ; and when I thought that the Wind would have shaken me from His Arms. Never for one moment can I forget how mighty He was in the midst of the Storm. How can I ever forget what I felt when He set me safely on the bank, and I saw the headlong River sweep onward harmlessly to the Sea ? Then, again and again, I have been with Him under the Palm Trees, by the Fountains. Weary and worn out, I have rested on His Sacred Heart. To me He is all in all. He lives for ever and ever ; and, while He lives, I see in Him all that I can seek. As I faint in this Desert, the very thought of His love is to me the shelter of a changeless rest. The shadow of my Home falls on me even here. I always call to mind the promises that He made. He promised to love me for ever. That promise is more priceless than all. But He also promised that I should be with Him for ever in His Home. He said that He was going to make ready a place for me, that where He is

there I also may be. Besides this He promised
to be with me always on my way. I know that
I can trust Him to the uttermost. I know that
His love for me is strong and deathless. I am
strengthened, enlightened, refreshed, comforted,
by that love. So, as I go along the weary way,
I call to mind all that He said. He told me of
His bright Home, the Home that He left when
He clothed Himself in poor raiment to seek for
me beyond the dark water. He told me of its
white Streets and its Flowers and its Fruits
and clear Stream and pearl-set Gates: and I
wondered as I listened. I said to Him, 'All
this wealth of blessedness and love can not be
for me;' and He said, 'Yes, My redeemed one,
for thee.' So I wondered still more. Ever since
that time I have thought ceaselessly about this
Home. Always the Shadow of its loveliness
falls on me here in my sorrow; and I sometimes
think that my heart will break with dreaming of
its brightness. I think too that I shall know it
when I see it, from what He has told me about
it. But, far more priceless than all, is His love.
This is my rest, my bliss, my life. His watchfulness is round me and above me; and I never
can tell a thousandth part of His love.' Thus

on her way she comforted herself with thinking
of the King: and thus, when she was far away
from the Palm Trees, she found the Shadow of
a Rock in the Desert.

Again and again the Princes of the King
heard her speaking to Him, and heard what He
said in answer, as she walked, lonely and sorrowful, over the blistering sands. Oftentimes what
she said was like this: 'Divine Love, I remember all that Thou didst give to me just now
under the Palm Trees; but the sun is so hot
that I am fainting by the way. I am not thank-
less for what Thou didst give me; but Thou
didst give me so much that I know that Thou
wilt give me more.' His words were ever
full of comfort; 'I am with thee in this Desert
always,' He said, 'and My love encircles thee
always.' I thought that she would have been
more comforted with this answer than she was.
She said, 'Dear Lord, the way seems so long, and
the heat is so great that I am almost fainting.
How shall I ever be able to reach the cluster of
Trees so far away? Divine Love, what shall I do?
They are so far off that my heart is failing me.'
No fretfulness ever wearied out the patience of the
King. 'Dost thou not know that I am with thee

always,' He said, 'and that My love encircles thee always?' This forbearingness took the repining spirit from her soul, and made her tell Him what she knew herself to be: 'Forgive me, Divine Love, for I am weak. I know that I am wretched, and poor, and miserable, and blind. I do not doubt Thee; how can I do so? I know what Thou art. I know what Thou hast done. But I am foolish and easily cast down; and in this heat my soul is dried up without Thee. Moreover that which Thou didst give me was so sweet, that I longed for it again, but not according to Thy Will. I cannot wish for it too much, but I must wish for it in Thy time, when it seems good to Thee to give it.' All this time the Princes of the King were listening with great joy, and they rejoiced still more when they heard Him say: 'I am always with thee and always give thee My love.' 'Thou art indeed ever with me, Divine Love,' the Bride said, 'and Thy Sacred Heart is to me a Shadow in the day-time from the heat. I can there find a shelter from the sun, even when I cannot reach the Palms. Thy love, ever with me, is my shelter. Thy Sacred Heart overshadows me, as I walk amid these sands. I kneel before Thee, and Thou art to me the

Shadow of a Rock. I see the glare of the sun on the sand around me: but Thou dost shelter me from it, so that it scorches me not. Thy love is my shelter in this Desert. Thou art my rest. Divine Love, so change me into Thy likeness and keep me in it, that my will, my heart, my life, may be ever pleasing to Thee.' Then I heard the King say, ' My redeemed one, once dead, now alive again, once lost, now found again, all that I have is thine.' These words comforted her as you may know from her answer : ' O Divine Love, I did not know what a shelter Thou couldst be from the pitiless heat. Now I know it and am glad. To Thee I can always turn, for Thou art ever with me. Like the Shadow of a Rock, Thy love saves me from the heat of the sun. Thou dost keep me from perishing. I kneel before Thee, and Thy shadow falls on me and I am safe.'

I saw that the radiant Princes always bowed themselves down before the King with the lowliest worship and with the deepest love, when His Sacred Heart was like the Shadow of a Rock in the Desert.

Thus on her way His Bride comforted herself with thinking of Him. All His great love overshadowed her, and filled her heart. She thought of Him, as He is, changeless in joy and beauty. She thought of all that He had done for her and of all the gifts that He had given her. But most of all she thought of that faithful promise that He would love her with an everlasting love.

She had also a great love for those Princes who stood round the King when He went out into the night : and who ever watched over her beneath the Stars. She was going to be with them for ever in the Home of the King. Most of all she loved the one Prince who ever stood by her with his silver Spear, watching over her and guarding her from harm. But all her love for others was as nothing to her love for Him Who carried her through the River in the drifting Rain. When she thought of Him she felt as if her heart would break with the greatness of its bliss. To Him she was ever lifting up her hands, and to Him her soul was ever turning. So she went on her way, thinking of Him, loving Him, trusting Him, waiting for Him, saying to herself: 'I am utterly unworthy of His love : there is nothing in me that can in the least draw Him to me; how is it then that He

loves me as He does? It is His own Divine
goodness that draws Him to me, for He loved
me long before I loved Him. Even when I
wandered from my Home into the darkness He
still loved me, and sought me, and came to me,
and drew me from the land of death. It is not
that I first loved Him, but that He first loved
me, and gave Himself for me. Great and
wonderful is His love; it is my bliss and my
life. How should I get through this Desert but
for Him? I could as easily have got through
the fierce River that drove onward to the Sea.
I shudder even now when I think of its headlong Stream. But now I know that He loves
me, and I know all that He has done for me.
He has gone into the Sanctuary of my heart
where none but Himself could go: for I was
created to love Him, and serve Him, and see
Him, and be with Him for evermore. There in
my soul He ever abides, living in me, and
making me strong. He promised that, if any
would love Him, He would love them in return,
and come to them, and make His abode with them.
But, every day, knowing what I am, I wonder
more and more that He can love me at all; still
though I wonder I do not doubt; for He told me

D

that He loves me, and I can trust Him to the uttermost. I do not doubt; for if I doubted Him I should die. I have been with Him under the Palm Trees and by the Fountains, and I shall soon be with Him again : but even now amid these sands He is with me, and His love cleanses me, and comforts me, and makes me strong. O my hidden Love, Thou art to me a River of Water and the Shadow of a great Rock in this Desert. Thou art to me a Tabernacle for a shade in the day-time from the heat.'

Thus she loved the King and talked to herself about Him. As He watched over her beneath the stars, in the midst of His Warriors, so He guarded her beneath the sun. His Princes too loved her with a great love as she went on her Homeward way. The sun beat fiercely on her as she went onward to the Cedar-crowned Mountains. There were Serpents in the Desert, and the heat of the sun was great.

The King was with her on her way; and her home was in His Heart. Whenever she thought of Him He was to her a shelter from the heat; the Shadow of the great Rock that stands up in the Desert land.

CHAPTER VI.

IN the Desert there were fiery Serpents, and poison was in their· bite. They glided swiftly, hither and thither, over the sand. The Bride of the King remembered how she had been bitten by them when she wandered from her Home and lost herself in the darkness beyond the River. She knew indeed that it would never be like that again if only she took care to keep herself in the Shadow of the Rock ; but, as she suffered from the heat, so she suffered from the bites of these fiery Serpents. Still they could only bite her so as to cause her pain, but not so as to carry her away again into the dark, because she was careful to keep herself in that Shadow which was to her a covert and a refuge. Any Bride of the King, when brought from the darkness and set in the Homeward way, could again, if she chose, go wandering back to the Plumes of Death beyond the River. But, as a matter of fact, this Bride, of whom I am telling you, never tore herself away again from the light, after the day when the King carried her in His strong Arms through the Torrent. They who were bitten in the heart passed away from the King into the dark: and there were many who were so bitten that they never came back from that outer darkness.

From day to day the Bride passed in the Desert many bleaching skeletons of those who had died from the poisonous bites of the Serpents. These skeletons filled her heart with a great fear; but that fear was her safety.

You may wonder how their skeletons were in the Desert, if they themselves were in the darkness beyond the River. I have just told you that some were so bitten that they did not come back from that darkness. They died on the spot beneath the fangs of the Serpents. For these the King sought, but they would not listen to His Voice; so, by their own will, they stayed in the dark, and their bleaching bones lay unburied on the sand of the Desert.

There was one Bride of the King who had gone through the Desert to her Home, without having been once bitten by the Serpents; but

she had never been beyond the dark River, and
had never feared lest she should be swept away
by its Waters into the Sea. From her steps,
as she went Homeward through the sand,
the Serpents fled away in fear. They could
not bear the Emeralds gleaming on her
Sandals.

But many, brought often from the darkness
beyond the River, at last died for ever by their
bites. The Bride on her way could see their
bones bleaching upon the sand. When the Serpents bit the heart of any Pilgrim, then came
death; either that darkness beneath the sable
Plumes from which they could come back; or
that last death when their bones lay in the
Desert, and the King never thought of them
again. But they never save once reached the
heart of this Bride of whom I am telling you.
She was indeed once away from the King in
the dark beyond the River: but after that her
watchfulness was so great that the Serpents
could only bite her feet. When her feet were
bitten the pain was not like the pain which
they felt whose hearts were bitten, but still it was
great: and when she felt it she understood the
blessedness of that Bride who, in her sweetness

and strength, had passed unharmed along the whole of the Desert-way.

Now there were two works of the King, which I saw, and at which I wondered greatly. The Serpents could not harm beneath the Palm Trees, nor beneath the Shadow of the Rock when it was deep. They were never in either place for long; nor so as to be able to bite. They lived in the heat of the sun, and they could not breathe for long in the Shade of the Rock: nor could they live long beneath the Palm Trees. So, if some Serpents found their way thither, they soon died. Indeed they could only bite even the feet of the Bride when the Shadow of the Rock was faint. When her heart was fixed on the King she was safe. This was one great reason why she always longed so earnestly to reach the Palm Trees. For though the Shadow of the Rock, according to the measure of her love, kept her safe, it was far easier for her to feel the King's Presence, when in deed and in truth He was with her by the Fountains of Water. Therefore with great gladness she always came to the waving leaves of the Palms.

But the King had done another wonderful

work. He did not leave her to herself when
He set her safely on the bank of the River and
told her that she must go through the Desert
to her Home. He remembered with a great
sorrow how He had seen her look when she sat
in her black raiment beyond the River that was
rushing on, darkly and fiercely, to the Sea. If
He had not loved her as He did, He would not
have stept down from the door of His Home
and taken His way through the night. If He
had not loved her as He did, He would not have
gone down beneath the dark waters when they
swallowed Him up. If He had not loved her
as He did, He would not have borne her back
through the Torrent when the Wind and Rain
were driven in His Face. But, as He loved
her so much, He could not leave her without
help among the fiery Serpents. He planted
the Palm Trees and made the Fountains of
Water; while the very thought of Him was to
her a shade in the day-time from the heat.
Thither the Serpents could not come to kill.
Beyond these shelters they were swarming, full
of venom, over the sand. So the King did
this other wonderful work of which I just now
spoke. Whenever the feet of the Bride were

bitten, a red Pool stood before her in the sand; and she stept into it, and the bite was healed. The water in the Pool was brought from the crimson Torrent through which she had been carried.

Thus then she went through the Desert trying to keep her heart always fixed on the King. Even when she was far away from the Palms she dwelt in the Shadow of the Rock, and thither the Serpents could never come death-laden. They could not even touch her with their venomous tongues in that Shadow when she made it strong by her love. So it was with the sun. The sun did not fall on her so as to do her any harm, when by her love she kept under the Shadow of the Rock. Nevertheless, even in the Shadow of the Rock, when it was not deep, the heat did fall on her so as to cause her some suffering. This was the Will of her Love. Thus as she went on her way the King was always with her, encircling and guarding her with His love.

Still the dread of these Serpents was a great pain. When they swarmed round her, her thoughts were always carried back to the storm that swept over the River. So when I first

heard what she said to the King among those
Serpents I did not quite understand her words;
but afterwards I understood them well. She
said; 'Merciful Love, the great Storms shake
me, and the great Floods overwhelm me. Sometimes it seems as if I must be borne away into
the Sea. I am almost deafened by the howling
of the Wind. I am almost blind with the beat-
ing of the Storm.' Now this made me wonder,
till I saw how the Serpents carried her thoughts
back to the River that nearly swept her away.
I heard the King say to her; 'If only thou
keepest hold of My Hand thou art safe.' Then
she answered and said, 'I know that, Eternal
Love, I know it and turn to Thee. I know
how weak I am and how strong Thou art. I
know that there are none like Thee in Heaven
or on earth. O that I had wings like a dove
that I might fly to Thee, and rest in Thy Heart.
There is my shelter from the storm of wind and
rain. I go into that shelter, and hide myself in
Thy Sacred Heart; and Thou, my crucified
Love, with Thy Own pierced Hands, dost shut
the doors upon me, as the fury of the great
Tempest rushes by.'

The King said, with gladness: 'As I made

a way for My ransomed through one flood, so I make a way for them through every flood, that they may be brought safely to their Home. Now I have hidden thee in My Heart.' Then she was heartened and said many words to the King; 'O Thou kind and pitiful One, let me speak to Thee for a little while from this shelter in which I am: and let me tell Thee about myself. Oftentimes I have forgotten Thee, and turned from Thee, and then my soul has been troubled greatly, and my life has been like the life of those who go down to the pit. But in the flood of great waters Thou wast my refuge, and didst give me understanding, and didst teach me in the way that I should go. My Love, it was often needful for Thee to rebuke me, but Thou didst not do so in Thy heavy displeasure; it was often needful for Thee to chasten me, but neither didst Thou do this in Thy anger. Thy arrows were fastened in me; Thy Hand was strong upon me; I was bowed down in my woe; sorrow filled my heart all the day; I was smitten and humbled very much; my heart was troubled; my strength forsook me; the light of my eyes was not with me.' Her sorrow seemed to me to touch the Heart of the King so much that He could not but speak to her words of comfort. I heard Him say in a voice of Divine tenderness, 'If your sins be as scarlet they shall be made as white as snow, and if they be red as crimson they shall be white as wool.' Full of hope because of this promise, she said, 'Merciful Saviour, Thou didst not stand afar off. Thy Ears heard me ; Thy Voice comforted me ; in my sorrow Thou wast stricken, and my chastisements fell upon Thee. How can I speak, Divine Lord, of Thy loving-kindness and pity? No one ever bore with me, ever loved me, as Thou didst : no long-suffering was ever like Thine. I sinned against Thee, and Thou forgavest me till seventy times seven times. I fled from Thee, and Thou didst take me in Thy Arms; I turned against Thee often, and Thou didst kiss me. Merciful Lord, Thy goodness saved me in spite of myself ; Thy beauty showed me my ugliness ; and the love of Thy Sacred Heart made me hate myself, and repent in dust and ashes. I never knew my utter worthlessness, my utter blindness, my utter darkness, till I saw myself in Thy light. When I wished to make my-self ready for Thee, then I understood how

wretched and blind and poor and naked I was.
Yet Thy love was so sweet and so strong, that
it transfigured me, and took me out of myself,
and lifted me up to Thy Heart. Thou didst
stoop down and didst find me in the dust, and
didst set me with Thy Princes. Divine Love,
Thou hast done far more than this: Thou hast
made me Thy Bride: and if I love Thee to the
end I shall be Thy Bride for ever. Divine
King, merciful and pitiful, how tender and for-
giving and gracious Thou art.' She now
stopped for a while, looking at the veiled Face of
the King. Then she looked down on the sand
and a shudder passed over her, and she said;
'O my Love, how dreadful these Serpents are.
They are so glistening, and their speckles are
so bright, and they glance about so quickly in
the white sand and in the glaring sun, that my
eyes are dazzled, and I can not see where to
step. My heart is full of anguish when these
fearful Serpents follow me. Their quivering
tongues are like weapons of fire on every side.
O help me, my merciful Love.' He answered
thus; 'I will be with thee through the fire; and
the flames shall not kindle upon thee. No
weapon that is formed against thee shall

prosper.' I thought that these words would have consoled her, but a greater shudder, as I saw, swept over her and she said, 'Merciful Love, let me not tread in the slime that they leave on their tracks; I can not bear it; it sends a shudder through my soul.' With the very look of compassion that was on His Face when He went through the River, I heard Him say; 'Look always at My Feet and Hands, once pierced for thee, and thou shalt be safe. Look always at My Side, wounded for thee, and I will keep thee from the destroyer. Enter into thy chamber, and shut the door upon thee, and hide thyself there till this agony pass away.'

When I saw how many were the swarms of these fiery Serpents, my heart seemed to die within me with a great fear. They clustered together in such numbers that you could scarcely see the sand. But, through the might of the King, their spotted bodies, glistening and slimy, were not to be seen, save sometimes for a moment, beneath the Palm Trees. They did not come, so as to able to bite, even beneath the Shadow of the Rock when it was deep. There they always seemed weak and languid. But they came in numbers where the Shadow was faint; and they covered the sand in swarms where the Shadow was not: then their bite was always poisonous and often deadly. If for a little while the Bride was where the shadow was weak, they bit her feet; but everywhere through the Desert were the red Pools of healing; and when she stept into those Pools the pain of the bite ceased. Very often the scars of those bites could be seen; but, sometimes, when her sorrow was very great they were quite taken away. It was not a matter of life and death to the Pilgrims to step into those Pools save when the fang of the Serpent reached their hearts: but, even when their feet were bitten, the red water in the Pools gave them great comfort and refreshment and strength. At times also the Shadow of the Rock was so strong that it kept the Serpents away altogether. But I will not say that she did not sometimes fear them greatly even beneath that Shadow. If she had not done so, she would not have been safe, for the King, her Love, had told her to fear them always. She knew that they would be a cause of fear to her even in the Orchard, beneath the golden-fruited Apple Tree; even beneath the

Yew in the Valley; even in the River through which she had to go. Beyond that River they could not pass. Not one could be found in the City of the King.

Now I think that you understand clearly how this was. You see that it was very much the same with these fiery Serpents, as it was with the heat of the sun. The Shadow of the Rock made the heat of the sun bearable. It did not altogether save the Bride of the King from suffering, for this was not His Will; but, as it grew deeper by the might of her love, it saved her so much from the sun's rays that, in one way, it is true to say that they could not pierce through it. That is what I mean when I tell you that the sun did not burn her beneath the deepest Shadow of the Rock; and that the shadow often kept the Serpents away. Thus the Bride of the King went over the sand, among the fiery Serpents: and often because of them her heart was full of anguish. The red Pools were ever to be found on her way. They were refreshing even in the sand, which sometimes was so hot that you could scarcely tread upon it.

Some of these Serpents were small, and

others were very great and fearful. They had
forked tongues, long and sharp. They had
speckled bodies, lithe and glistening, and hideous
heads and slimy feet. Their feet were slimy
even on the hot sand. That was one of the
things at which I wondered most. If ever the
Bride of the King trod on the slime, as she
went barefooted through the Desert, it made
her tremble, and sent a shudder through her
soul.

These Serpents greatly dreaded the silver
Spears of the Warriors of the King. Still
more they dreaded the emerald Sceptre of the
one Bride who had passed unharmed through
the midst of them, from whose steps in Shoes
they had always fled in dismay. No one, you
must remember, ever went in Sandals through
the Desert, save only that one Bride whose Feet
even were never bitten by the Serpents. All
others went barefooted over the sands. As they
went she gave them great help ; far more help
even than all the Princes together could give
them. When you saw the Princes in their
gleaming beauty, a great Army which no
man could number, you could not help wondering at the power of the one Bride over whom

the sable Plumes had never waved. There were myriads of the Princes, like flames of fire: but she was far mightier than they. So the Serpents greatly dreaded her Sceptre. But most of all, of course, they dreaded the Arm of the King, Who had carried His Bride through the Torrent from the Land of Death ; Who gave her rest under the Palm Trees ; Who was to her the Shadow of a great Rock in the Desert way.

They always fled, swiftly and in great fear, from the very foot-prints of those Feet through which the nails had been driven.

CHAPTER VII.

As the Bride went on her way she had a ceaseless sorrow in her heart. Even in the Shadow of the Rock she felt it, and beneath the Palm Trees it dwelt with her. At times that sorrow was so great and its sharpness so keen, that the tears trickled down her cheeks. Then the King and His Warriors loved her more than ever.

Now her first great sorrow was the remembrance of the sufferings of the King. She sorrowed for His pain, remembering all that He had undergone in that time of darkness when He carried her through the Torrent in the midst of the Storm. She could never forget that hour; and the remembrance of it was printed on her heart. Before her in memory there ever stood the Torrent and the Rain and the strong Wind and the Plumes of Death ; and through it all there shone like a star the love and strength of the King. She remembered the anguish of His Heart as He went on His way to find her, and that made her sorrow for Him on her Homeward path. In memory she ever mingled her tears with His, and, as she went onward, never forgot the sharp thorns through which He had gone. In all this there was great pain, but there was comfort beyond the pain. She said to herself, 'If He had not loved me as He did, He would not have suffered for me thus. If I had not been so dear to Him as I was and am, He would not have gone for me through such a Torrent and such a Storm of Rain. I can tell His love by His sorrow, by the anguish of His Heart. How He must have loved me when He went out into the night. How He must have loved me when he went down into the Torrent, and its waters swallowed Him up. How He must have loved me to come to me among the Worms and Creeping Things, when I was bitten by the Serpents.' Then again she said, 'It is indeed a pain to think of the misery that I brought upon Him; and yet but for this I should never have known the greatness of His love; but for this I should never have seen that wondrous look on His Face, when He went onward in the greatness of His strength.

Now for evermore that look is enshrined within the veil of my heart, in its Holy of holies. No one can come to that Sanctuary but Himself. No feet but His have ever trodden it, or ever can. My whole heart and all my soul go out to Him when I think of His love. They go out from me and lie before Him in love and worship.' Often, by a sort of fascination, she returned to the thought that she would never have known how the King loved her, but for the grief that she had brought upon Him. Then in a moment she was overwhelmed with pain to think of all the suffering that she had brought on One Who loved her with such a deathless love. Thus she called to mind the suffering of the King, and mourned for Him with a great mourning, and sorrowed for Him with a bitter sorrow.

The next great reason of her sorrow was that she was away from her Love. Lonely and weary, she passed onward to her rest. Over the sand, among the clusters of the Palms, with a sorrowful heart she went towards her Home. Though the great Rock overshadowed her, yet her Love was hidden from her eyes. She ever kept saying to herself as she went : ' My Beloved is to me a Bundle of Myrrh ; one day He will be a Cluster of Cyprus, but now He is a Bundle of Myrrh ; and thus He lieth always on my heart through this dark night of my pilgrimage and sorrow.' So she passed on her way. Faithful and trustful, she bore up against the sun, and passed amid the Serpents, and lifted her eyes to the Cedar-crown on the far-off Mountains, and wished for her Home on Libanus with the King. Who can tell the sorrow of her heart in those days of waiting when she was parted from her Divine Love? She could think of nothing but Him, and could long for nothing but Him. Yet she did not see Him ; and the road was very long and dark.

As she went on her way, she ever said to herself : 'When shall I see His Face? When will He bring me to my Home? How long must this darkness last? When will this journey end? When shall I be with Him for ever, and never go away from Him any more?' This being away from the King was the second great sorrow of the Bride.

Another great sorrow was her knowledge of her own unworthiness. She knew that, when she had done all things that He had commanded her,

she was only an unprofitable servant. She
knew also that she had nothing but what He
had given to her. Ever more and more with a
great knowledge she felt her own meanness and
poverty and darkness. Ever more and more
the King, her Love, stood before her with a
brightness and strength that made her veil her
eyes. Thus her spirit ever longed to be more
clothed in white, and she said, ' I must love and
adore Him at a distance; I am not worthy to
lie at His Feet.' This however was not the
Will of the King. He said to her, 'Not at My
Feet, but on My Heart.' So she had to clothe
herself in white and make herself ready for Him
that she might be His Spouse for ever in His
Kingdom. It was for this that He had come to
seek her in the darkness of the night : for this
that He had borne her up with such a strong
right arm, through the waters of the flood.
Feeling this she said, ' How can I ever make
myself ready for Him ? How can I ever be clad
in my Marriage-Garment ?' Then the King
Himself taught her that He sought only for her
love. He said to her, ' Give Me thy heart.'
He wanted nothing but that ; and it was only
by this that she could ever be brought into His

Presence, in the midst of His Princes. If she loved Him she could not help doing all that He wished. She took comfort in this, knowing that every thing which she had was His gift. As it was His Will, she desired to lie on His Heart, though she knew that she was not worthy to kneel at His Feet. His Will was her will, whether it lifted her higher or set her lower. She always lay in spirit at His Feet. This was gladness of heart to her. It was her happiness to lie there in uttermost adoration : and to feel that she was nothing and that He was all in all. Perfect obedience came from her love, and that obedience was pleasing to Him. She loved Him and obeyed Him in all things : and always rejoiced in giving her obedience, as He rejoiced in having it. This lowliness of spirit brought her peace. It made her say again and again, ' I must love, with all my heart and soul, Him Who has such a love for me.' So she was not utterly cast down with a knowledge of her own unworthiness.

Also she had a great sorrow for those who were away in the darkness, beyond the River and beneath the sable Plumes. With a great desire she was always praying that they might be brought back and set once more in their

Homeward way. But she had no sorrow for
those whose bones were bleaching in the sand as
she passed. The King had no sorrow for them,
and His thoughts were hers. All things made
her strive more earnestly to do His Will and
reach her Home.

Thus she journeyed onward from one resting
place under the Palm Trees to another; and
passed on beneath the Shadow of the Rock;
and went safely amid the Serpents, as the sun
fell upon her and the sand blistered her feet.
She ever sang to herself as she went: 'My
Beloved is to me a Bundle of Myrrh. He is
lying on my heart all through the night of my
sorrow.'

Now it seemed to me that sometimes the
weariness of the way was so great as to constrain
her to cry out to Him, and tell Him of her
sorrow. I heard her speak to Him like this:
'O Lover of my soul, I cry out to Thee in my
anguish, and I lift up my hands to Thee. The
storms go over me, and I am afraid. Hast Thou
set me in the darkness; and wilt Thou not let
Thy light shine? I am weary with crying and
my throat is dry. O Divine Love, comfort me
in this greatness of my sorrow.' When she said

this she was crying bitterly in the anguish of
her heart : but she was comforted when the
King said : 'I have graven thee upon the palms
of My Hands.' Still her sorrow and fear came
back, and she answered : 'Thy Hand lieth
heavily upon me, and Thy arrows are fastened
in me. I am wretched and bowed down ; I walk
in sorrow all the day long. Thou hast smitten
me, and I am afflicted : Thou hast set me in a
thick darkness, in a living death. Lord, all my
desire is before Thee, and my groaning is not
hidden from Thee. My heart is troubled ; my
strength has left me ; the light of my eyes is
gone. Forsake me not, O Lord, my God ; do
not Thou depart from me. Give me Thy help,
O Lord, Thou God of my salvation. In Thee,
O Lord, have I hoped ; Thou wilt hear me, O
Lord, my God. I am weary and worn out with
waiting so long upon my God.' Then the King
speaking with a gentle voice said : 'I will have
thee in everlasting remembrance.' She was not
yet consoled, and said to Him most sorrowfully :
'Deep calleth to deep ; I lift up my hands to
Thee. O God, the deep of my woe calleth to
the deep of Thy mercy, and I lift up my hands
to Thee. My eyes are dim and my heart hath

failed me. I lift up my hands to Thee. The
storms pass over me. The noise of the waterfloods makes me afraid. Fear and trembling
are come upon me, and darkness hath covered
me. Divine Love, I lift up my hands to Thee.
I call to Thee out of my sorrow. My heart is
aching with sorrow. I must kneel down, and
tell Thee of the anguish of my heart. O my
Love, what can I do? How can I go on? O
comfort me, my Love, in my sorrow.' Then He
said in a voice of Divine gentleness; 'I will
comfort thee with a great comfort in Jerusalem:
and the voice of My people shall be the voice of
joy and praise.' Yet once again she answered
and said : 'The arrows are sharp : they have
pierced me. The iron has entered into my soul;
and I am troubled in my sleep. The sorrow of
my heart hath bowed me to the ground, and
there is no strength in me. I am wasted away
with grieving, and Thy Hand presseth me sore.
My way is strewn with thorns. I am feeble
because of the terror of the day : I tremble
because of the horror of the night. In great
fear, in the heaviness and anguish of my soul,
my merciful Creator, I lift up my heart to Thee.
Pity me and help me, O God of my salvation.

Help me, my God and Father, to wait till the
end comes: then bring me to my Home.'
Again over the sand came the voice of the
King : 'I will comfort thee with a great comfort
in Jerusalem. Mercy shall be built up for ever
in the Heavens; My truth shall be made ready
in them. I have loved thee with an everlasting
love, therefore I take pity on thee.' You will
think that the Pilgrim ought to have been comforted by this : but it was not so ; and she cried
out: 'My soul is filled with sorrow: my life
fadeth away to the grave. Sometimes I feel
tempted to say, 'This sorrow is too great for
me; I cannot bear it.' The world is darkened
for me; the light of the stars is hidden ; the
moon hides her face; the sun does not shine. I
say 'How is all this to be borne? Who will
strengthen me? I am sick at heart and stricken
and crushed and ground to powder between the
upper and nether mill-stones.' O Divine Love,
hear me, and be merciful to me, and take pity
on me, for I am desolate with a great desolation,
and sorrowful with an overwhelming sorrow.
Still in this darkness of my spirit I look up to
Thee, my Comforter, and see Thee, and trust
Thee, and love Thee. Joy is not for me till I

see Thy glory; and from me the light has gone till Thou comest in the breaking of the Day. I am waiting till Thy Home be revealed in its beauty. There I shall be at rest and there my sorrow will be healed. I am looking onward to Thee, as my tears fall, as my weary feet bear me Homeward. Thou, my merciful Love, wilt one day give to me the sleep which Thou givest to Thy beloved. Even now I am reckoned as one of them that go down to the pit : I am become as one without help. I am as one of the slain sleeping in the sepulchres, whom Thou rememberest no more. They are cast off from Thy Hand. I am hidden in the lowest deeps, in the dark places, in the shadow of death. Divine Love, out of my sorrow, I lift up my heart to Thee. The darkness enfolds me, and the Cross bears me down to the ground. I cannot look up. I bow myself in the dust, and the hurricane shakes me as it passes. There is a sharp pain in my heart that nearly kills me; and the shadow of a great dread hangs over me. I almost say to myself, 'O that I might lie down and die and be at rest.' But, Divine Love, though Thou shouldest slay me, yet will I trust in Thee. Thou art kind and merciful; and I give myself to Thee, and ask Thee for Thy help, for Thou knowest my misery. Yet always in these deeps of sorrow I love Thee; and lift up my heart to Thee. Help me my merciful Love.'

The King was divinely patient, and was never wearied out. This was His answer: 'My redeemed shall return and shall come into Sion, singing praises. Everlasting joy shall be on their heads. They shall be filled with gladness: and sorrow and mourning shall flee away for ever. I, I Myself, will comfort you.'

Then His love and patience triumphed in her heart and gave her peace. All darkness passed away, and the light poured in upon her soul. She rejoiced with a great joy, even in the sufferings which were sent to her by Him.

Thus from one resting place to another she went Homeward through the Desert; but, as I have already said, a ceaseless sorrow filled her heart. Beneath the sun and the stars her Beloved was to her a Bundle of Myrrh. She longed to be with Him in His Home. Her soul seemed to die within her, when she was away from Him. As she went along in the darkness she used always to think of the light shining from the lattices of His House. She

felt that she would gladly walk as far as her
feet would carry her even to see a glimmer of
that light. Most of all did she long for her
Home, when she was most weary at heart. She
said, 'O that I had wings like a dove, for then
I would fly to my Love, and be at rest.' Her
eyes were ever lifted up to the light shining
beyond the flood. Still she went patiently along
the Desert-way : for she knew that this was the
Will of the King. Her sorrow in many ways
was very great, but she always remembered that
she had brought it on herself. She remembered
also that she had brought His great sorrow on
Him, and that was the most piercing thought
that she had. She never forgot the fierce River.
Always there stood before her a memory of the
Plumes of Death beneath which she seemed to
behold her Love coming to her in the darkness,
with a look of agony on His careworn Face.
This made her say to herself, 'It is only right
that I should have this sorrow ; but He was
sorrowful through me.' Indeed when the heaviest
sorrow bowed her to the ground she never had
against Him one rebellious thought; though
sometimes, I must acknowledge, she seemed,
in words at least, to be complaining of

the crosses that He sent. She well knew that
nothing but good could ever come to her from
Him. Of that there could be no doubt. She
could not always understand what He did, but
she always knew that all that He did was good.
She sometimes had to go through the dark, but
she knew that it was so in order that the light
might be brighter at the last. Whatever, therefore, her Love did, she never had one distrustful
thought, one thought that was disloyal or un-
loving. Her soul went out from her and lay at
His Divine Feet in love and worship. In her
heart she carried the knowledge of His unself-
ishness, His pity, and His love. Again and
again as she was thinking of Him and loving
Him, as she was thinking of her Home and
longing to see it, there came up to her an echo
of the rushing of the great River sweeping
onward to the Sea. Sometimes on her way
through the Desert she came near to the shore
of that Sea. She saw its white-crested waves
lifted up in their strength; and often watched
for long, gazing on it and thinking of her Home
and her Love: saying to herself, 'Can He in
truth know how I love Him for all that He has
done for me? Can He know how I love Him

for His Own goodness ?' Then with great gladness she felt in her heart that He knew and
understood her love : and this knowledge was
to her a joy which ever brightened the darkness
of the way : and helped her to go through her
sorrow patiently onward to her Home.

The Princes loved her as she went. In their
strength and majesty they guarded her,
sometimes with their flaming Swords, but often-
est with their silver Spears. Then she heard
faintly the sound of the great Battle that never
ceased. Very often the way seemed to her as
if it would go on for ever, as if the rest would
never come ; but then she said, ' The longest
road and the longest day must have an end.'
Very often she said, ' I would rather have all
this sorrow with Him than every gladness
without Him. If there be no other way of
having His love except by this suffering,
then I willingly choose it and rejoice in it. I
would not be without the bitterest grief that has
ever come to me, or can come, if I could only be
spared it by the loss of His love.' Very often
she also said, ' Besides I must not forget that I
can lighten my suffering and at times get rid of
it altogether by telling Him about it. If I

speak to Him only in my heart the pain goes away. He seems to be near me, and I do not feel it. When I tell Him of my sorrow, such a Divine love falls on me that I rejoice in all my suffering, however great it may be, because of the love that I get through it. In Him I have a boundless trust ; and the more that I trust Him the more I feel that I can trust Him utterly. Though my sorrow is so great; yet this trust is such a blessing that the only way in which I can thank Him for it is by silence and tears.' Then again she said, ' I could not go on without this love and pity. Without Him I could not bear this pain; but with Him I can bear all sorrow, and rejoice in it, whatever it may be. I am of good cheer because He has overcome. Now I am sorrowful, but my sorrow will be turned into joy. I shall see Him one day and then my heart will rejoice ; and no man will be able to take away that joy from me. I shall be with Him where He is that I may see His glory.' These thoughts helped her to go patiently on her way. Indeed, in one sense, it seemed nothing to her to wait for Him. The years were only so many days because of her love. Every hour she thanked Him that He

F

had given to her the blessedness of waiting. If she had chosen for herself she would rather have gone to Him at once, but that was not His Will; and His Will was her will, always and in all things. She thanked Him, therefore, for letting her wait. In another sense every day was a year, because He was away. But she never murmured, for His Will was best. She always looked on to the Orchard; and, through the dark Valley, to the Garden of Lilies. She knew that He had espoused her to Himself; that one day He would bring her to the Altar on Libanus; and that then she would be with Him for ever in the Light. In great sorrow then, yet in great joy, she said to herself on her way, 'In the dark night my Beloved is a Bundle of Myrrh to me, lying on my heart.' Even as she said it in her sorrow her heart was filled with gladness: and she went onward, full of hope, to her Home in the City of the King.

CHAPTER VIII.

As I have told you, the Bride rested from time to time beneath the shadow of the Trees that grew by the water. There the King always came to her and gave her rest. Then even in the Desert she had the prelude of those joys which ear hath never heard, and eye hath never seen. In those meetings she saw His Face dimly and darkly, not as she would afterwards see it in the light of that Home to which she was going. Still she saw it more plainly than when He came to her beneath the sable Plumes, or when He bore her through the River. Her love taught her to know His Face, and understand every look that it ever had.

Now she had always known that she had to go through a Valley that was very dark and a River that was very cold, before she could reach the Garden of Lilies. The King had said so. She knew also that He would come to her for the last time beneath the Palm Trees that grew in the Orchard. There was a little clump of Palms after you passed the Apple Tree and before you got to the Yew that stood at the entrance of the Valley. I will tell you about the Apple Tree and the Yew presently. When the Desert way was all but ended the King came to His Brides beneath those Palms for the last time before the going down into the River.

Now the Orchard stood on the outskirts of the Desert, on the right, just before the Valley began. Indeed you first caught sight of the Orchard and the Valley almost at the same time. There her Desert-journey would end. She knew that the end must come, but she could not tell when it would be. She had often said to herself when she went out into the Desert from the Fountains of Water, ' I wonder if this will be the last time. Perhaps it will be in the Orchard that I shall next be with the King.' Still she could not tell; she never asked Him about it. Even when she loved Him most and when He gave her the greatest gifts, she never asked Him, for it was not His Will that she should know.

But she understood His looks; and one day

after being with Him she could not help speaking to herself and saying : 'I do not know what it is, but I cannot help feeling that I have been with Him beneath these Desert Palms for the last time. I think that He will next come to me in the Orchard, and then under the Palms that are growing there. He did not say anything to me about it ; but I think so from a look that I saw on His Face.'

As she said this the sun seemed hotter than ever and the sand more scorching than ever. She heard also more clearly the rushing of the River as it went downward to the Sea. That sound came up along the road that she had gone. She was close to the Sea, gazing on its waves, when she heard that sound. She was wondering where that Sea ended and what was in its searchless depths ; what was the meaning of its murmur, of its ripples, and waves, and flakes of foam. Suddenly there fell on her ears the rushing sound that she had heard so long before, when she sat beneath the Plumes of Death. Then also she heard for the first time the flowing of another River ; but that sound came to her from the Valley beyond the Orchard. That was the Valley to which she was going. It

was the same kind of sound as that which had
filled her ears when she was carried through the
Torrent, but it was not so loud nor so fearful.
She knew therefore that the River to which
her steps were leading her was not so strong
as the River through which she had been borne.
Still her heart seemed to die within her.
Yet the King had never seemed to her so full
of love, as when she saw the look on His Face,
that told her of the Valley through which she
must go.

Now also she heard far more plainly than
ever the sound of the great battle, that I have
spoken of before.

On, then, she went, walking more than ever
in the Shadow of the Rock. That Shadow, as
I have told you, was not like the Shadow of the
Palms; for it was the love of the King as she
thought of it in her heart, and not His very
Presence. Under the Trees He came to her in
truth and deed. Still that Shadow of the Rock
was full of comfort; and it had never been so
great as on this day, when she thought that she
was coming to the Orchard. She knew too, you
must remember, that in the Orchard would be
growing the Palms beneath which the King

would meet her for the last time ; the last time, that is, while she was in the Desert.

Now she did not know for certain that she would be there before the evening. It was only a feeling that she had ; but it turned out to be true. For as the gloaming began to draw its veil over the world ; as the heat of the sun was dying away ; as the fresh breeze crept over the sand ; she lifted up her eyes, and the Orchard, of which she had been so often told, stood before her in its sweetness and its beauty.

The Evening Star shone above it, and a gentle wind came to her, fragrance-laden, over the hedge. Then she knew that she must go very soon through the Valley. Her comfort in that hour was to know that she could lean on the Staff of the King. She could fear no evil, for He would be with her, coming to her in the Orchard with such love as even He had never given before.

A flood of joy swept through her soul when she knew that the journey was all but over. She said, 'Now I am going to my Love.' She said, 'Soon I shall see Him in His beauty.' She said, 'Soon I shall be with Him in His Home.'

Then she knelt down, and lifted up her
hands to the King, and said ; 'I thank Thee,
Divine Love, that I am coming to Thee at last.
I shall soon have peace and gladness ; and
sorrow and mourning will flee away.   Thy
Face will fill me with light.   I shall have joys
from Thy right hand and shall drink of the
torrent of Thy pleasure.   With gladness and
rejoicing I shall be brought into Thy Temple.'

She rose and passed on with her Olive-branch
in her hand into the Orchard.   The light of an
Autumn-sunset fell on the Flowers and the
fruit-laden Trees.   Her gray Hood and Cloak
shone through her Veil.   The sun was very low
in the heavens, when she went into the Orchard,
seeking for her Love.

The Trees were laden with their treasures.
White blossom had turned into fruit, purple and
red.   The pink bloom of the Almond Trees
had faded long ago, even before the leaves
had unfolded themselves fully ; and now the
Almonds were hanging on the boughs.   The
Apple Trees had been deckt with rose-pink
and white ; but then their branches were bowed
earthward with red and golden Apples.   Among
the Trees many Flowers were growing.   The

Honey-suckle was interlaced with Jessamine in
the hedge that surrounded the Orchard, and
their sweetness filled the air and was borne onward by the gentle wind over the Desert. The
lilac Mallows were there. The ox-eye Daisies,
like the sun, stood up in their loveliness. Mea-
dow-sweet grew there with its feathery sprays.
There the Cuckoo flower, pinkish or silver-white,
flowering longer than its wont, seemed as if it
were made for the clothing of that one Bride of
the King whom the Serpents could not touch.
There too were St John's-wort, and Sun-roses,
with yellow or white bloom, and stately Bell-
flowers, and lingering Violets with their little
purple blossoms.

In the midst of the Orchard rose up an
Apple Tree, fragrant and golden-fruited. It was
laden with apples, and scented the evening air.

The Bride of the King, in her dark Veil, in
her Hood and Cloak of silver-gray, passed from
the Desert to the Orchard, through the Flowers,
beneath the heavy-laden Branches; and sat
down, weary and footsore, under the golden-
fruited Tree. There the King came to her;
and there she was with Him in that last twilight
before going down into the River.

Never had He been so gracious as He was on that evening in the Orchard; and never before had He given to her such treasures of His love. His Coming then was far more even than His Coming under the Palms. As His Warriors, set in array, had always stood round Him beneath the shadow of the Palms, so now more brightly than ever they girdled that Apple Tree like a wall of fire. Still dimly, yet more clearly than before, she saw the Face of the King. There was a look upon it, like that well-remembered look, printed on her inmost heart, that she had seen in the Rain. She now had to go through a River, little indeed in itself, yet great for her; little indeed, and yet like that crimson River, strong and fierce, through which she had been borne. Now she had to go by herself; and yet not alone, for the King would be with her, though she could see Him not. He had come to her now to say to her the words which no one but Himself could say, and to strengthen her, as no one but Himself could strengthen her, for her going down into the Valley of the Shadow of Death.

The Evening Star shone over the head of the King, as He sat beneath the Apple Tree. A

gentle wind mingled its fragrance with the scent
of the Honeysuckle and Jessamine in the hedge,
and bore it onward over the sand. As it passed
it stirred the leaves on her Olive-branch.

The Apples and the Almonds were laden
with fruit, when the King came to His Bride
at the end of her long journey.

The Evening Star shone brightly over the
Apple Tree as it stood in the midst of the
Orchard. Beneath that Tree and beneath that
Star the King was sitting among His Princes.

As I looked, one of those Princes came and
took me by the hand, and led me nearer, till the
branches of the Apple Tree hung over my
head. Then I heard these words ; 'My Saviour,
Thou didst bear the burden for me, and for me
Thou didst go through the heat of the day.
Very long and very hard was Thy journey.
Thy bleeding Feet and tear-worn Face tell me
of Thy love and sorrow. For me Thou didst
go down into the lowest and darkest deeps of
anguish and shame. For me Thou didst drain
Thy bitter Chalice to the very dregs. If thou
couldst have shown me Thy love more by going
into darker and more fearful depths Thou
wouldst have gone. Boundless and everlasting,

O Divine Saviour, is Thy love for me. Trustfully I rest within that love, and the storm touches me not. I am hidden in my chamber and the doors are shut, till the blast of the terrible ones shall pass away for ever. Thou didst keep the great Cross for Thyself, and in Thy love Thou hast given only a little Cross to me.' The King, sitting beneath the Apple Tree, answered her and said ; 'I love them that love Me, and they that seek for Me early shall find Me.' She knelt down before Him with her eyes full of tears, and kissed His Feet, as her tears fell on them, and answered Him thus ; 'Yes, Divine Spouse, Thou lovest all Thy creatures who are away from Thee ; and then in Thy love Thou bringest them back to Thyself. Thou didst even die for me when I was Thy enemy. Greater love hath no man than this, that a man lay down His life for His friends. Thou didst die for me when I was not Thy friend, that Thou mightest reconcile me to Thyself. But, my merciful Saviour, I must speak the truth to Thee ; and tell Thee that the Cross which Thou hast given me, though it be little to Thine, is very great to me; for it sometimes bows me to the ground and

crushes me and almost breaks my heart. Thou
knowest it, Divine Love; Thou wilt not love
me less for saying so; for Thou dost take great
delight in the trustfulness of Thy creatures.
Yet I have rejoiced to have that Cross; and I
would not have parted with it for all else that
could have been given me. My weakness sometimes made me shrink from it; but I always
loved it in my heart. Still, as Thou well
knowest, I have sometimes been hardly able to
carry it, and bear up under it, and follow Thee
along the Desert-way. Sometimes I have been
tempted to say, 'This is more than I can bear.'
Sometimes, I fear, I have said it; and then Thy
love hath heartened me, and Thy Arm hath
strengthened me, and Thou hast said to me
sweet words about the rest that Thou wilt give
me on Thy Heart. I have often fainted beneath
the weight of my Cross; I have often shrunk
from the rod of Thy discipline. In weariness
of soul I have gone on my way; often fretting
and murmuring, and grieving Thee. But now
I can rejoice for all that Thou hast done, for all
that Thou hast sent. The shadows are passing
away from me, and the light gets clearer, and I
can see better than I did. Thy way is in the

great deep and Thy footsteps on the mighty
waters : but, Divine Love, that great deep and
those mighty waters are now growing bright
with the glimmering of the Day.   Thou hast
brought me to the end of my journey ; now
Thou comest to me Thyself, more lovingly than
ever.   O Lover of my soul, I never dreamed
that it would be like this.   How could I know
about such joy as this, till it came ?   How could
I dream of this fulness of Thy love ?   I knew
what it was to be with Thee under the Palms ;
and I always thought that from those times I
should know about this time.   But now I see
how little I knew, and how poor my thoughts
were.   Now I see that I did not know in the
least the blessedness of being with Thee here
in this Orchard.   How gracious Thou art ; and
how sweet Thy fruit is to my taste.'

She was kneeling at His Feet while she said
these words.   In His graciousness and kindness
He stooped down and raised her up, and said to
her ; ' In that day I will be a crown of glory, and
a garland of joy to the residue of My people.'
' Thou hast carried me in Thy Arms,' she
answered, ' and on Thy Heart, Divine Love, to
this end of the way ; and Thou hast helped me

where I never could have helped myself. Thou
hast borne with me as no one but Thyself would
have borne with me. Compassionate Saviour,
I should have wearied out any love but Thine ;
Thou canst not be wearied out : and Thy mercy
and long-suffering grew, as it seemed to me,
with my darkness and want of love. When I
think of all this, Divine Spouse, it makes me
love Thee more.' Upon this the King said,
looking upward to the Cedar-crown on Libanus ;
'Judgment shall dwell in the wilderness and
justice shall sit in Carmel. The work of justice
shall be peace, and the service of justice quietness and security for ever. My people shall sit
in the beauty of peace, and in tabernacles of
confidence, and in wealthy rest.' When the
King said this, a light passed over her face, and
all the Princes, as I saw, rejoiced greatly. She
was beginning now to get glimpses of their
silver Spears as they watched over her. With a
smile on her face, and the tears running down
her pale cheeks, she knelt again and looked up
to the King and said ; 'Thou hast done every
thing for me, my Saviour and my King : Thou
hast done every thing for me : and for this I
thank Thee and for this I love Thee. Thou

didst once tell me that if I did all the things that Thou didst command, I should still be unprofitable, still unworthy of Thy love: but, O Thou merciful Saviour, what must I call myself, when I have done so little? Now in the greatness of Thy love Thou hast come to me, and here Thou givest me the fulness of peace. Thou hast brought me into Thy Orchard that I may be strengthened to go down through the Valley into the River that I must pass. My Love, how can I thank Thee? I cannot thank Thee at all. I can only kneel at Thy Feet, and look up in Thy Face through my tears. O Thou Lover of my soul, I thank Thee for all Thy gifts; but most of all I thank Thee for bringing me safely to this hour in which I am coming to Thee. Now be with me, Divine Love, more than ever, for now, more than ever, I need Thy help. I hear the noise of the great battle raging beyond that Hedge, and I should be frightened, if I were not with Thee. Thou, in Thy love, dost save me from all fear. Thou dost keep me in perfect peace, for my heart is stayed on Thee. With Thee I dwell in the security of rest.'

It seemed to me that the King grew brighter and more loving every moment. His Voice was most sweet and solemn as He said ; 'The land that was desolate and impassable shall be glad ; and the wilderness shall rejoice, and flourish like a lily. It shall bud forth and blossom, and shall rejoice with joy and praise. The glory of Libanus is given to it, and the beauty of Carmel and Saron. They shall see the glory of the Lord and the beauty of God.'

Such words as these fell on my ears, as I stood beside the Prince who led me into the Orchard. I can not tell you how majestic the King was, beneath the Apple Tree, when the Evening Star was shining, and the sunset-glow was dying away in the sky. In beauty and graciousness He stood there as He had often stood under the Palms. Yet now He came even with deeper love, and with greater gifts. He had Himself gone through the Valley and the River ; had Himself heard the wailing of the Wind and felt the icy coldness of the Water ; and therefore His Heart was filled with great pity for her who had to go down into the Valley and through the River. So He was more gracious than ever when He came to the Orchard.

Very sweet was the scent of the Honeysuckle and Jessamine that came from the Hawthorn-

G

hedge on which the red Berries were shining.
The South wind was blowing through the
Orchard; and again it stirred the leaves of her
Olive-branch.

As she rested there she looked back on her
long journey through the Desert; and tried to
count up the times that the King had come to
her under the Palms. When she thought of
those times, and dwelt on them in her heart, she
saw very clearly what He had been to her and
what He had done for her. He had always
been the same as now, for He could not change;
and yet there seemed to be a difference. It
seemed to her as if His love were deeper and
stronger than ever, now that He had come to
her for the last time to strengthen her for her
going down into the River that must be passed
before she could reach her Home. As she
knelt before Him in the Orchard, near the
cluster of Palms, beneath the Apple Tree over
which the Evening Star was shining, she could
just hear the noise of the River at the bottom
of the Valley. For a moment, as she heard it, a
great fear smote her. She put back her Hood
from her ears, and listened, that she might hear
the sound more plainly, and be able to make out

what it was like. The evening glow ˉwas in the
sky ; and the last rays of the setting sun fell on
the braids of her golden hair. It was well indeed
for her that the sound came to her in the Orchard
when the King was with her. If she had been
by herself she would have died of fear.

You must, I think, be glad to know that now
her journey is all but ended ; and that the sands
will never again blister her feet. When she
heard the sound, and turned to her Love, and
looked up at Him, and spoke to Him, her face
was pale, and her voice trembled. But it was
only for a moment. All her fear vanished,
when He spoke to her words of comfort, and
promised to be with her, even though she could
not see Him, on the dark way along which she
had to go.

Then, as ever, His Princes were there : and
the points of their Spears were glittering everywhere among the Trees of the Orchard. They
were all round me where I stood, so that I could
touch them as they passed. But most of them
were beyond the Hedge, in the Desert, warring
against the dark Legions who had always been
seeking the destruction of the Bride. That
conflict, as you know, had always been going on

from the beginning; and the Warriors of the
King had always guarded His Bride with their
silver Spears : but now for the first time she
begins to hear the noise of the Battle very
plainly, and to see it very clearly, as if she were
in the midst of it herself. The confused noise,
loud and fierce, came to her in the Orchard;
but she knelt there peacefully at the feet of the
King.

As she rested there, and heard the sound
of the River, it seemed to her as if the old
time had come back again, when the King
carried her through the crimson Waves, and
bore her in safety to the Bank. Now she
has to go down into another River, that she may
reach another Bank on which ever shineth the
brightness of her Home. She said to Him,
looking up so trustfully into His Face that it
would have brought the tears into your eyes if
you had seen it: 'My Loved One, is this the
great River rushing onward, of which you told
me? Is this a breath of the strong Wind, that
I remember so well, in the old days, sweeping
up from the Desert and the Sea?'

As I looked, I wished with all my heart that
I could help her: but I could not. She must

needs go through the Valley alone ; and her only
help would be the unseen Hand of the King.

Refreshed and strengthened, she rose up and
went on her way towards the Valley, as the
Princes of the King gathered in the Orchard.
The light of the setting sun fell on their Shields
and Armour and golden Helmets.

The Cedar-crown on the Eastern hills stood
out clearly before her as she went. I had never
seen it so well, nor had she ever had such a
sight of it before. Once again, for the last time,
she found the King beneath the Shadow of the
Palms. Never before had His lips dropped
such choice Myrrh, and never before had His
Hands been so full of Hyacinths.

There was a rustling of the leaves ; but the
birds were silent on the branches. The noise of
the Battle again rose on her ears, as she went
towards the Hawthorn-hedge. Thus in the
deepening twilight she rose up as the Evening
Star was shining, and went towards the Valley.
Her Hood and Cloak did not shine so plainly
through her Veil as before : still you could just
see the glimmer of the silver-gray. Her face
was pale but calm. She had her Olive-
branch in her hand as she went. I knelt down

and prayed that she might pass safely through the River.

She went through the Hedge of May and saw the dark-green Yew that stood at the entrance of the Valley. The Rocks with their glossy Ivy rose up on each side. She looked upon the Yew, and said: 'I have passed from the Palms to the Apple Tree ; I must now go beneath the shadow of that Yew. It is the Will of my Love.'

The twilight was still deepening : but her Olive-branch was tipped with light.

A mournful Wind stirred the branches of the Yew.

CHAPTER IX.

RISING up she went towards the Valley and the River. With the love of the King in her heart she left the Orchard and came to the rugged Cliffs between which she had to pass. The farther that she went the stronger and brighter grew her love. She came to the Rocks. They were reddish-brown, and were covered, here and there, with masses of dark Ivy. High on both sides of the dim Valley they stood up, steep and fearful.

At the entrance to the Valley was a Yew, dark and solemn. Beneath its flaky branches it was dark even in the twilight. Countless ways, as it seemed to me, led up to that Yew; but only one way went onward from it. The Pilgrims going homeward travelled by that road.

With her Olive-branch in her hand she stood beneath the Yew in the gloaming, and gazed earnestly down the Valley. Her eyes seemed deeper and brighter than ever as she gazed. The gloom was so thick that she could see but little. The cold wind rising up from the Valley struck her and made her shiver. She heard the rushing of the River; and for a second her heart failed her; and she said 'I must go back; I cannot go on down this dreadful place; I would rather be in the Desert beneath the burning sun.' Then the King spoke to her; and she felt His Hand taking hold of hers in the darkness; and her spirit within her lived again and she went on. Round her were many of the Warriors of the King with their Spears and Swords.

Thus in the twilight, beneath the Evening Star, she went from the cluster of Palms in the Orchard towards the Valley. The horror of a great darkness lay upon that Valley; and for a second the rush of the Torrent smote her heart into trembling. But it was only for a second. Very easily frightened about other things and at other times, she never felt any fear about things that had to do with her Divine Love, nor when she was with Him. The very thought of the King, much more His presence, gave her new life and new heart. Greatly did she wonder at this. At other times dangers made her afraid, but dangers did not seem to be dangers when

He was near. All things were transfigured by her love.

As she stood beneath the Yew, gazing wistfully down the Valley, she trembled for a moment and then said, 'Divine Love, how heavily the branches of this Yew hang over me. I cannot see a star through the great flakes of green, and the waving of the branches fills me with awe. All through the Desert I have known that I must come here at last ; I have been making myself ready for this time all through my journey, and now it seems as if my heart would fail me. All the days of my life I have been waiting for this change. Now it is coming ; and I am afraid. Though it was so near, yet for a little while I forgot it in the Orchard with Thee, for Thou wast with me. When I am with Thee, I forget everything except Thyself. But, O, how different is the waving of this Yew from the waving of the Palms ; from the waving of that Apple Tree, where I have been just now with Thee.'

Then I felt the icy wind come up from the Valley : it seemed to creep into my bones, and chilled me to the heart. When all was darkest I heard the voice of the King coming past the Ivy and the Rocks. He said, 'In all sorrow I am thy joy; in all darkness I am thy light; in the gloomiest way My Hand shall guide thee; in every hour of danger and distress I am thy only Comforter; I will give thee everything that thou needest; beneath this Yew Tree I am with thee.' These words strengthened her, as I could see, and she answered, 'O Divine Love, no words can ever tell how I love Thee for all Thy care of me; for all Thy goodness to me; for all Thy watchfulness over me. Thou art like none else, and none can be like Thee. Whenever I think of truth or justice, I think of Thee, for Thou art the only just and the only true. Now I need Thy love as I never needed it before; and Thou wilt give it as Thou hast never given it before. The more that I need Thy love, the more Thou dost always give it. O my Love, with what a trust do I say to Thee all that is in my mind, and tell Thee all my thoughts. As I talk to myself, so I talk to Thee. I am afraid of all others, but I am never afraid of Thee. Help me now, Divine Love, in my hour of need.' An answer of comfort came from the King, as the branches of the Yew waved over her in the twilight : 'Though thou comest with weeping I will bring thee to Myself in mercy; I will guide thee in the right way, and thy feet shall not stumble. With great joy thou shalt come to the place which I have made ready for thee.'

As soon as she heard these words, she went with unfaltering steps from beneath the Yew into the cold Valley and the gloom that stretched away to the River.

A mist rose up from the Valley, and the cold struck her again and made her shiver. Jagged Rocks cut her feet and made them bleed. She tried to see through the mist, and dimly she saw a dark River like that through which the King had carried her. Frowning Rocks, covered here and there with patches of Ivy, rose up on each side of her way. The wind moaned through that waste land, and the cold struck her a third time, and her heart was like ice. But she felt the Hand of the King, and was strengthened and went on. The twilight made the Rocks more fearful, but she went on. Her feet were torn by the Flints.

Many Flowers grew on the Rocks, where the Ivy did not come, and close to the path along which she went. There were Plume-thistles, and Dead-nettles, and scarlet Poppies, and the large bells of the Thorn-apple, and the purple

berries of the Deadly Nightshade. There also
grew Henbane with its clammy leaves, and
venom-scented flowers, cream-coloured, with
their network of purple veins. There were the
crimson-spotted stems of the Hemlocks ; and
Hellebore with dingy-red edges on its green
flowers, and acrid Spurge with yellowish-green
blossoms, and Wolf's-bane and Aconite, both
with helmet-like flowers, one yellow and the
other leaden-blue. It was just light enough for
her to see this.

Dimly, in the twilight, she saw also many
skeletons of Pilgrims who had perished. The
Valley was strewn with bones, and these Flowers
were also growing among them, as well as on
the Rocks. In some places they reared their
heads in the skeletons ; among the bleaching ribs, or through the holes in a skull, where
eyes had once been. Hideous little reptiles too
were crawling through the sockets, and that,
I thought, was as ghastly a sight as I had
ever seen : for those eyes could never look on
the King in His beauty.

Strange faces peered out upon her as she
passed : and hideous monsters with skinny hands
threatened her in the gloom. Great bats, very

fearful to see, were flying about; and they sometimes struck her with their wings as she passed.
One frightful beast struck her such a blow that
she fell. But she kept hold of her Olive-branch:
and the Hand of the King lifted her up. Now
she heard more plainly the rushing of the River;
and the cold grew more piercing. The darkness
came on apace. At last she saw nothing but
the overhanging Rocks. No trees nor flowers
grew in that part of the Valley to which she had
come. The Ivy did not grow there, nor Hemlock,
nor Poppies, nor the Nightshade, nor any of the
flowers that I mentioned. But strange faces,
with an unearthly light in them, peered on her
through the darkness, and frightened her. Great
toads, and blind-worms, and snakes, and many
hideous Reptiles crawled round her feet and
sent a shudder through her soul. She knew
that they were the fiery Serpents under another
form : but she felt the Hand of the King taking
hold of hers in the darkness and she was
heartened and went on. That Hand guided and
helped her on her way. Without it she could
not have gone on, for it was so dark that she
could not see. The icy wind, far colder than
ever, pierced into the very marrow of her bones.

Always when her heart began to fail she stooped down and kissed the Hand of the King : and she was strengthened and comforted. Her Olive-branch touched her cheek, as she kissed His Hand. She felt it, but she could hardly see it, for the light all but faded from it. for a little while, and the darkness was very dark. She heard more plainly the moaning of the Stream and the wail of the Wind as it came up between the Rocks. She could not see her hand before her face. This I was told by one of the Princes of the King, for it was so dark that I could not see.

As she went down the Valley she saw the Warriors moving hither and thither through the gloom. An unseen light, oftentimes, lit up their Shields and Helmets, and then the whole Valley was bristling with Spears. Their Shields and Helmets, again and again, gleamed in the unseen light : but brighter than all were the tips of their silver Spears.

The Wind was blowing so wildly and so drearily that it seemed like a wail of grief for her sorrow and pain.

With her Olive-branch in her hand she went on through the darkness, down the Valley. The Rocks stood up on each side.

As she went on she spoke to the King in a very low voice, and said, 'This icy Wind brings over me such a coldness that my heart is frozen within me. O, compassionate Love, this Valley is very dreadful. It is far more dreadful than the Desert in which I have been so long. These Rocks make me afraid. These Flowers are not like those that I saw in the Orchard; and these Creeping-things curdle the blood in my heart. Fearfulness and great trembling have taken hold of me.' Then again came the Voice of the King; 'My Elect shall not labour in vain, for they are the Blessed of the Lord. I will hear them when they are yet speaking; and even before they call on Me I will hear, and will answer.' The darkness now seemed to grow much thicker, as I heard her say; 'O, Divine Love, how fearful this darkness is. I am treading on sharp stones, for I cannot see them: and they cut my feet. Now I cannot see even the Flowers that I saw when I first came into this Valley. I can scarcely see my hand before my face. These over-hanging Rocks seemas if they would crush me. I can see them very dimly in the darkness; but I feel that they are hanging over me. That faint streak of

light in the sky shows me how high they are,
and how nearly they meet over my head. I
cannot see one star in that dim streak of sky.
O my Love, merciful and pitiful, be with me in
the horror of this darkness. Strengthen Thy
loved one now in this hour of her agony. Now
I cannot see my hand before my face. Now I
can hardly see any light in my Olive-branch.
O, merciful God, strengthen and guide Thy
loved one in this agony of death.'

Nothing could be thought of more divinely
tender than the words of the King; 'Though
thou art walking in the midst of the Shadow of
Death thou must not fear, for I am with thee.
My Rod and My Staff are thy comfort now
My mercy shall follow thee to the end of thy
days, that thou mayest dwell in the House of
the Lord for ever.' Then these words fell on
my ear; 'Divine King, I can feel Thy Hand,
or I could not go on. Thou art leading me
and comforting me, and Thou wilt bring me to
the Lilies. The thought of Thy Lilies and
Pomegranates, of Thy Palms and Cedars on
Libanus, upholds me now. I can go on
because I hope to see the Altar in Thy Temple,
and the River ever flowing through the City

of Thy love. But these jeering faces and this flickering light make me shudder; once I nearly let my Olive-branch fall from my grasp. Put Thy Hand before my eyes that I may not see them : let me feel it upon my face. Be a shelter to me, my merciful Love, for the Wind is colder than ever : and I hear the rushing of the River far more than I have ever heard it as yet. O how clearly the noise of the battle rises on my ears. My Love, help me on my way.'

The Rocks, high and craggy, on each side of the Valley, seemed as if they would fall on her and crush her as she went between them. She had passed far beyond the Yew; no trees, no flowers, were there : and if there had been any she could not have seen them, so thick was the darkness. In one place, as I said, and as you also know from her own words, it was so dark that she could not see her hand before her face. She trod upon ashes; and there were sharp Flints scattered among them, and those Flints cut her feet. The ashes on which she trod, crumbling beneath her feet, reminded her of those that had once been sprinkled on her and round her, when she sat in her sackcloth, beneath the Plumes of Death. Mocking voices,

H

harsh and shrill, rang in her ears. Hideous forms, lit up with a pale light, loomed on her through the mist. Jeering faces peered at her from the crags. But she kept tight hold of the unseen Hand of the King, and they did not frighten her then. A great bat just then struck her, a second time, with its wings, and made her stagger. Strange Reptiles swarmed round her in the ashes among the Flints, and crawled over her feet. Because of this, every now and then, a great shudder swept over her, and a great loathing filled her spirit. At times she felt as if all her flesh were creeping. Some of these Reptiles she could not see, but some of them glistened faintly. These had forked tongues, sharp and poisonous. Some of them were small and hideous, and some were large and hideous : but all were full of deadly poison, and if they could have bitten her heart she would have died then, and gone for ever into the dark, even though she was so near the end of her journey. The Pilgrims whose hearts were bitten in the Valley or the River died for ever, and never were brought to the light again. The King had no time in which to seek them. They dwelt for ever in the outer darkness, which is far more

fearful and far more full of anguish, even than
the darkness beneath the sable Plumes. This
was the time when the bite could be given from
which no pilgrim could recover.

At the entrance to the Valley, in the gloaming, she saw, as you remember, many skeletons
of Pilgrims who had died there from the bites
of the Reptiles, just as she had seen so often in
the Desert the skeletons of those who had died
for ever from the bites of the fiery Serpents.
For these Pilgrims there was no more hope;
nor could they ever come back again to the
King. Many of those whose hearts were bitten
in the Desert, and who were carried into the
dark, came back and set off again on their
pilgrimage. But some were so bitten that they
never returned; though the King was always
ready to bring them back, if they wished.
These left their skeletons on the sand. Thus
they were like those whose hearts were bitten
in the Valley. All the Pilgrims, indeed, had to
go through that Valley and through the River.
But their skeletons were left in the place where
they were so bitten by the Serpents as to come
back no more from the darkness. Nightshade
and Henbane and Spurge and Hellebore and

Hemlock and Poppies grew among their bones. In many places also the bones were lying scattered about. When she came to the part of the Valley where the flowers did not grow, and where it was so dark that she could not see, she felt the bones beneath her feet. Sometimes she stumbled over a skeleton, and would have fallen if the Hand of the King had not held her up. Even there the Creeping Things could bite her; but there, as in the Desert, were the red Pools of healing up to a spot fixed by the King. When you passed that spot those who were bitten in the heart could not be healed. She could always tell where the Pools were, even in that thick darkness, by the light that shone from them and hovered over them. That light was very different from the phosphorus-like glow that covered the Reptiles. She could not, however, be quite safe till she had passed the appointed place.

Again and again, as she went on through the gloom there rose upon her ears the sound of the war which she had heard in the Orchard, when she was under the Apple Tree. She had often heard the same sound faintly in the Desert. Indeed I hardly can say whether it was hearing it or not: but, at any rate, the farther she went down the Valley, the oftener and more plainly she heard it.

All around her, and up on the sides of the Rocks, were the Warriors of the King. Their Spears and Shields and Helmets gleamed every now and then with light, though the brightness that lit them up was unseen.

Her right hand was stretched out; for with that hand she kept hold of the Hand of the King, whom she could not see. If you had not known that the unseen Hand of the King was clasping hers, you would have wondered why she kept her hand stretched out before her as she did. In her left hand was her Olive-spray. It shone with the same light as that which gleamed from the Pools of healing, and from the Armour of the Princes. At one part of the Valley indeed, as you will remember, all had been so dark that she could not see her hand before her face. That was the time when hardly any light fell from her Olive-branch. Now the gleam of that branch of acceptance fell through the dark on her face, and lighted her Hood of silver-gray and her Veil. The rays of that light spread themselves out, so that you could see them piercing the gloom. She went on, and passed out of the Valley to a Plain through which the River was flowing. The darkness began to grow a little lighter. Just as she was getting over some loose stones that lay between the head of the Valley and the Plain, a nameless thing, loathsome and slimy, flew at her heart and threw her down. She fell, full-length, on the stones. They were very sharp, and had jagged edges. She was not hurt: and the hideous beast was suddenly flung far away into the darkness. Through the gloom she saw the Hand of the King. When she got out to the Plain she turned and looked back on the Valley and thanked Him with her whole heart. Then with new hope she looked on and saw the River. It was flowing between her and the Garden of Lilies, and there was no way for her to that Garden save by passing through its waters. There was, indeed, another River, but it was of fire; and over this River there were Bridges, by which, without touching its waves even with their feet, Pilgrims could go to the King's Palace. Very few Pilgrims, however, entered His Garden without going through that River of Fire,

Beyond the River she saw the Mountain
with its Cedar-crown, which she had seen often
on clear days while she was in the Desert.
She went on towards the River. It was still
twilight for her ; but beyond a Hill, which
hindered the light from coming to her, there
was brightness in the sky. So I was told by
one of the Princes, for I could not see it myself, as I was standing on the Plain. Chosen
Warriors with silver Spears stood in two lines of
light from the end of the Valley to the River.
At a little distance, on an upland, were the
rest of the Princes. They were beyond the
Hill : and there, as I was told, the day was
bright. These rode on Horses : but the Spearmen who guarded the Bride were on foot. Their
backs were turned to her as she went downward
to the River ; for with their Spears they had to
guard her against the onsets of the Warriors
with black Armour and Plumes, who sought
ceaselessly to compass her death. But two
other lines of Princes with golden Helmets
stood with their backs to these and their faces
towards her, unarmed, with folded hands, watching her lovingly and reverently, as she went to
the River. There was only a spear-length

between these two lines. Thus there were four
lines of golden Helmets and two of silver
Spears from the head of the Valley to the
River. Between the two lines of unarmed
Princes the Bride passed over the Plain. As
she went they all loved her with a great love.
It was like the time when, in their midst, the
King had borne her up the Bank from the
crimson Torrent.

The twilight still rested on her : but beyond
the Hill, as I have just told you, there was
light on the Plain. Can you see her going
towards the River? If you can not see her,
come a little further from the Desert and a
little nearer the Garden of the King, and you
will see her plainly.

Calmly and fearlessly, through the twilight,
she went towards the River. Swiftly and
silently, that great River flowed onward to the
Sea. Drearily and wildly, the Wind sounded
in her ears. Above it she heard the noise of
the battle and the snorting and the rushing of
the Horses. She heard it indeed very plainly
now. Yet calmly and fearlessly, through the
gloaming, she went Homeward. She had hold
of the unseen Hand of the King. She said,

'O if I could only die for Him.' She said, 'I love Him so much that the only relief I could have for my love would be to die for Him. But He will count this wish as if I were dying for Him. He knows my longing and He takes the will for the deed.' She said, 'O my Love, I shall soon be with Thee for ever. O Divine Love, let me come nearer, nearer, to Thee.'

There was a great stir on the upland beyond the Hill. One of the Princes had now set me where I could see this. Masses of Warriors with black Armour charged the Army of the King. Dark Squadrons rode down on the lines of silver Spears that guarded the footsteps of the Bride. They came past the Hill into the twilight.. Their black Horses with flaming eyes and flowing manes, looked very fearful as they thundered over the Plain: but not a thrill of fear touched the heart of one of the King's Princes. Even if any fear had come to them, you could not have wondered at it, for nothing can be thought of more dreadful than the rushing of those sable-plumed Squadrons, as they swept over the Plain, fearlessly in their stormy grandeur, furiously in the fierceness of their strength.

All through the pilgrimage of the Bride there
had been war between the Warriors with the
golden Helmets and the Warriors with the sable
Plumes. It began in the Dark beyond the
River. It ceased for a little while when the
King was carrying His Bride through the
Torrent, for then the Beautiful One walking
in the greatness of His strength was Alone,
and got the victory with His own right
Hand. A great silence then hung over the
wonder-stricken Armies. The conflict began
again with renewed fury. It raged round the
Bride as she slept beneath the Stars, and as she
went over the Sand. There was an impenetrable line of Spears round the clusters of Palm
Trees and the Orchard. The Apple Tree was
girdled with a wall of fire.

With daring worthy of a better cause, yet
always unavailingly, the dark Army now spent
its strength against the lines of light. The
battle had begun to grow more deadly, as I told
you, than it had ever been before when the
Bride was in the Orchard. Then she began to
hear its noise very clearly. Indeed up to that
time, though she knew of it well, for the King
had told her of it, she had not heard it very

plainly. Beneath the Yew the noise grew clearer, and it increased in clearness all the way as she went down the Valley.

Now on the Plain beside the River was fought the great battle, and there was won the crowning victory of the war. Now she not only hears the confused noise, but sees with her own eyes the grandeur of the strife.

In this battle of which I am telling you, nearly all the Warriors on both sides rode on Horses. Those only were on foot who stood with their silver Spears or with folded hands on each side of the Bride as she went down to the River. All the Horses in the dark Army were black as coals; but in the Army of the Day some were white and some were red. All the sable-plumed Warriors had Visors: but there was no Visor in the Hosts of the King. There also the King Himself took the command of His Army. His Bride had been with Him beneath the Palms and the Apple Tree: and then, in the great conflict raging round the Orchard, His elect Princes led His Host against the ranks of Death. Now He is girding Himself with His Sword on His Thigh, for the day of vengeance is in His Heart. Though He is

girding on His Sword, though He is Himself
going down to the great battle-field, He will not
this day strike a blow with His Own Hand.
He won His mighty victory long ago in the
crimson Torrent: and, but for that victory and
for His presence, girded for the battle, there
would be no victory for His Princes now. His
jewelled Helmet, like many Crowns, is on His
Head, and He is girt with His golden Girdle.
In His Helmet is a Plume, white and ruddy.

His Bride must go down alone into the River ;
but do you think that I can rightly call it alone,
when He, though unseen, will always keep hold
of her hand, as He did when she was going
through the Valley ?

She passed onward to the River, in the
gloaming, between the lines of Spears, as the
dark Squadrons began to ride down on the
Army of the King. The dawn brightened a
little more in the sky. Her Olive-branch was
greener and fresher than I had ever seen it
before, save in that hour when she took it
from the Hand of the King. A brightness fell
from it. Her gray Hood and Cloak began to
grow whiter, and to shine through her Veil.
The Wind came up from the River with a

mournful sighing ; and over the Desert and down the Valley there reached her an echo of the strong Wind that the King heard when He was watching her beneath the Stars; that she had heard herself, in the old time, sweeping up from the Desert and the Sea. She knew that the Palace and City of the King were beyond the dark water: she could not see them, but dimly through the gloaming she saw the Cedars that were waving over them. The River flowed between her and the Cedar-crowned Mountain. Only through that River was her Homeward way.

The Armies were gathered ' together to battle, the number of whom is as the sand of the sea. And they came up on the breadth of the earth and encompassed the Camp of the Saints and the beloved City.' ' Behold a white Horse ; and He that sat upon Him was called Faithful and True, and with justice doth He judge and fight. And His Eyes were as a flame of fire, and on His Head were many Diadems, and He had a Name written which no man knoweth but Himself. And He was clothed with a garment sprinkled with blood, and His Name is called, The Word of God. And the Armies that are in Heaven followed Him on white

Horses, clothed in fine linen, white and clean.'
'The kings of the earth and their armies
gathered together to make war with Him that
sat upon the Horse and with His Army.'

Amid the noise of the battle and the neigh-
ing of the Horses, she passed without hurry and
without fear, in her innocence and graciousness,
downward to the River.

The dark Warriors knew that their time was
short, and according to this knowledge was the
fierceness of their onset. As the King loved
His Bride with a great love, so the leader of the
rebel Army hated her with a great hatred ; and,
with unbending heart and far-reaching wisdom,
sought to kill her. Never had he put forth
such strength as now. His mightiest Princes
led the forlorn hope of his Army on that day.
His Standard was black, like the gloss of a
raven's wing, and on it was a Wolf in red. He
himself rode a great Horse with eyes like
furnaces, and his deeds of daring on that field
surpassed his old renown. Wherever the fight
was thickest, the danger greatest, the onset
fiercest, there was that black Horse and his
Rider with the blood-red Plume. His Warriors
held back from no danger, but at his bidding

dashed themselves like tempest-driven waves against the Spears of the Defenders of the Bride; against the Squadrons of the Host on white Horses; against the unconquerable Warriors of the King who were charging them with their flaming Swords.

They knew that their time was short; and they swept like a hurricane across the Plain. On their black Horses they thundered over the ground, and flung themselves on the ranks of the King. Madly and fiercely, with the wildness of despair, they hurtled against the Warriors with the golden Helmets. But skilfully as they wielded their iron Spears and Swords; fearlessly and recklessly as they hurled themselves on the lines of light; they did not and could not change by the breadth of a hair the impenetrable array of those glittering Spears. Again and again they were broken and flung back from the Army of Light. Again and again they came down with new strength, with new fierceness: but it was all in vain: and again and again, bleeding and baffled, they were hurled back.

Thus the battle raged long and fiercely, with confused noise and burning and fuel of fire.

Great gladness filled my heart when I saw
the unavailing rage of the Army of Death.

The Bride was now near the River. A smile
of triumph began to light up her face. Her Hood
and Cloak grew whiter every moment, and her
Olive-branch shone more brightly. Calmly and
fearlessly, she went Homeward amid the din of
the battle. Yet now and then, as she caught
sight of the dark water rolling swiftly onward,
the shadow of a great fear passed over her
heart.

Just at that moment she saw a wondrous
sight that filled her heart with gladness. She
saw it like a glimmer and then it passed away.
The King gave her that glimpse to strengthen
her heart. I will tell you, as well as I can, what
she saw.

Near her on a rising ground was the flower
of the Hosts of the King, and in the midst the
King Himself. In His golden Helmet like
many Crowns, and only in His, waved a Crest.
All those in the Army of the Night had sable
Plumes, except their Leader, and his was blood-
red ; but no Warrior in the Army of Light had
a Plume. So, too, the King's Helmet was not
like the others, but looked, as I have said, as if

it were many Crowns. The Princes with Him
on that rising ground were His most elect
Warriors. They had white Horses like the
Horse on which He was sitting, and were without Spears; but in all His Army there were no
such flaming Swords as theirs.

There were Seven of them brighter and
stronger than the rest, and they were nearest to
the King. In each of their Helmets blazed a
Jewel. Their Armour too was not like the
burnished Armour of the others. Four of them
had Coats of Mail like fine brass burning in a
furnace. The Jewel on each Helmet of the
four seemed to me to be almost as large as a
pomegranate, and shone, brightly-flashing, like
fire. In one Helmet was a blood-red Sardius;
in another a Chrysoprasus, golden and green;
in the third a Chrysolite like fine gold; and
in the fourth a violet Amethyst. These four,
though they were greater than all others in the
bright Army, yet attained not unto the first
three. One of the three had Armour, red like
the crimson Torrent. In His Helmet burned a
Jasper, marked with red spots and white lines,
very piercing in its brightness. The next had
silver Armour, white and glittering; and in His

I

Helmet was a dazzling Emerald · like those on the Sandals of the Bride who went untouched by the Serpents along the whole of the Desert-way. The first and greatest was the Leader of the Hosts of the King All his Armour was of the purest gold. In his Helmet was a Sapphire, flashing and gleaming like the sun.

In their strength and trustfulness, in their fearlessness and beauty, they sat on their white Horses round the King. In their hands were their Swords, drawn and hanging down by the flanks of their Horses. Like the other Warriors, they had no Visors. In the midst of them was the Standard. It was of Cloth of Gold, and on it was a Lamb among Lilies and Pomegranates in white and scarlet and green. Round the Lamb there was a Crown of Thorns. The trappings of their Horses were far the finest in that mighty Host. The rays of the sun were now falling upon them over the Hill, and all their Armour glittered. It was the light that had fallen on the Helmets of the King's Warriors in the dark Valley. Brightest of all was the gleam of the Jewels in the Helmets of the Seven.

This is the sight that rose before her for a

moment, and then passed away. It filled her
with hope, and she went on cheerfully because
of this glimpse that she had of the strength
and beauty of the Army of her Love. She was
now on the Bank of the River; but though the
Dawn was brightening in the sky she was still
in the gloaming; and the rays of the sun did
not reach fully over the Hill to the place where
she was. In the dimness she was looking on
the dark River as it flowed. For a second the
shadow of a great dread passed over her.

It was at this time that she got leave from
the King to go to His Garden without passing
the River of Fire. She kissed His hand with
such great love, and with such great sorrow for
all that she had done in any way against His
will, that He promised to take her straight from
the River to His Home.

Onward rolled the battle between the Warriors
with the golden Helmets and those with the
sable Plumes. Fiercely the dark Squadrons
dashed themselves against the Army of light.
Recklessly, they plied their iron Swords and
Spears. The battle raged fiercely. Fearful
was the strife on that ever-memorable day.
Everywhere, in the midst of the black masses,

like lamps amid the darkness, were the Princes
with their flaming Swords. Everywhere in the
thickest of the fight on his dreadful Horse was
the Leader with the blood-red Plume.

All the time that the battle was raging, picked
Veterans of the dark Army were furiously
charging the ranks of the Spearmen who held
the passage of the River for the Bride.

On the mound, of which I told you, the King
sat on His Horse among His Princes; and His
Helmet, like many Diadems, was glancing in
the morning sun. He was clothed in fine linen,
stained with blood. The Garment that He
wore had been sprinkled with blood in the
crimson Torrent. His Sword was on His
Thigh, and in His right Hand He held a
Sceptre.

Onward rolled that great battle of the
Warriors. They covered the Plain beside the
River. Mighty and beautiful was the King.
Among all His Princes there was no one to be
found like Him.

One radiant Prince had never left the side of
the Pilgrim from the beginning. She had often
felt his presence, and he had often helped her;
but now for a moment she saw him and spoke

to him and went on with new gladness in her heart. This was another token of the kindness of her Love.

All the time, though she could not see Him, He was close at her side, and again and again she bent down her head and kissed His Hand as she went. But for His might she would have fainted by the way. Her Olive-branch always grew fresher when she kissed the Hand of the King.

At last when the time was come He sent His seven Princes with His elect Warriors into the battle. As they went down from that Hill, on their white Horses, with their flaming Swords, they looked like the Sea of Glass mingled with fire. In their starry brightness they shone among the sable Plumes. In the mightiness of their strength they clove the dark Legions as a great ship cleaveth the waves on which rest the shadows of the night. Their Leader, with the golden Mail and the Sapphire in his Helmet, singled out the Leader of the Army of Night and rode straight at him. In his strength and brightness, sternly and calmly, with a flush of righteous anger lighting up his face, he turned not aside to the left hand or the right, but went straight at the Warrior with the blood-red crest. Further and further through the iron Swords he rode onward in his wrath. The sable Plumes went down before him, as the long grass goes down before the scythe of the mower. It went through my soul to see the sweep of his flaming Sword. My whole heart was bowed down before him, as the brightness of his god-like beauty streamed out into the darkness of the strife. My spirit drank in the gleam of his radiant Armour. Nearer and nearer the Rider on the black Horse saw the glancing of the Sapphire. Nothing could turn aside the Prince in the golden Mail. As a river-horse crashes through the reeds of a jungle, so did his uncon-quered Horse bear him through the thickest ranks of the sable-plumed Warriors; through the darkest storm of their wintry Swords; through the closest array of their iron Spears. The Leader with the blood-red Plume saw him coming : saw the flashing of his Sword : saw through his Visor the gleaming of the Sapphire. He saw him coming, and he trembled. Nearer and nearer through the iron Spears rode that Prince in the splendour of his resistless strength. The mightiness of his own spirit carried him

through the breakers of that sable-crested Sea.
He was alone among those black-armoured
Warriors, ploughing His way, resistlessly and
calmly, through the waves of death. The rest
of the chosen Warriors were not near him.
Even the six Princes, his friends and com-
panions, could not keep up with him on that
day. His gleaming Horse bore him onward.
The Leader of the dark Army saw him coming :
saw the flash of his golden Armour and the
splendour of his flaming Sword : saw through
the bars of his Visor, nearer and nearer, the
burning of the Sapphire. Then a strange feeling smote his stormy heart. Like destiny, that
gleam of the Sapphire bore right down upon
him ; and he could not face it. Still fiercely he
led on his mighty Warriors : and wherever the
fight was thickest there was the blood-red Plume.

Now he is coming down with his Reserve.
All his chosen Veterans are round him. Thus,
for a little while, he is far from all the white
Horses, and it is through his bravest Warriors
that the Rider in the shining Mail is cutting
his victorious way. Like one great flake of
foam, white and dazzling, on the black waters,
he is alone in that weltering sea of sable Crests.

Like a pillar of fire rising through a dark wood of pines his golden Helmet gleams amid the forest of iron Spears. The sweep of his avenging Sword is like the forked lightning in the fury of a storm at night. Never has there been anything more terrific than the charging of those coal-black Horses, the biggest and strongest in all the Army of Death ; but through them all, without a pause, without a check, gleams the brightness of the Prince with the burning Sapphire above his brow. The dark Leader sees him coming : and he can not bear it. Still fiercely and dauntlessly he leads on his Warriors. But he quails before the flash of the Sapphire. Onward through the forest of death flashes the Rider in the gleaming Mail. The red-plumed Leader sees him coming resistlessly through the iron tempest.

Thus when the time was come the King sent down His chosen Warriors into the battle. As they went over the crest of the Hill, as they swept down its sides, as they charged over the Plain, in the splendour of their beauty, with their white Horses, with their glittering Armour, with their flaming Swords, they were like nothing, that I know of, but the Sea of Glass mingled with fire. They went down to the battle. Their Swords burned like lightning : and there was the brightness of a most holy anger in their faces, as they swept down on their foe.

The dark Legions stand aghast at the resistlessness of their charge. They stand aghast and waver. They tremble and are broken. The golden Helmets sweep on. The dark Legions are astounded ; and are smitten. Their ranks are riven. They reel and stagger. They reel and stagger ; and are scattered. The white Horses sweep on. As the dry branches of a forest that has been burnt with fire are broken off and scattered by a winter hurricane, so are the Warriors of the Army of Death scattered before the gleaming Princes of the Army of the King. The white Horses and golden Helmets sweep on.

The King is there in His deathless beauty. In His Face is a light of triumph and of gladness. The day of the great vengeance has come. The Helmets of His Princes shine among the sable Plumes like stars in the blackness of the night. Through their Visors the dark Warriors see them and are swept away. In vain they struggle against the victorious Princes.

They are ridden down by Troops and Squadrons and Divisions. The flaming Swords burn and flash among their black Helmets : the hoofs of the white Horses tread them down.

All the Host of the King is like the Sea of Fire ; but amid its splendours there is nothing like the gleam of the Jewels in the Helmets of the Seven. The Warriors on the black Horses are swept away by the waves of the Army of Light, just as you have seen the white breakers in a storm sweep masses of dark tangle and drift-wood resistlessly along the beach.

Thus the " land-wave " rolled on. The white Horses of the King with their Riders went down to the battle : and the black Horses and Warriors of the Army of Death were swept away.

Never had there been such a fearful strife as this : never had there been so utter a rout since the first great conflict of the war. The first battle and the last were the greatest.

The King looked with joy on the great battle raging in the light ; looked down also through the gloaming on His Bride as she stood between the lines of silver Spears on the brink of the

River. Then more firmly than ever He kept
hold of her hand.

At last the noise of the great conflict died
away and the Princes of the King moved from
their impenetrable ranks. After the battle the
Leader of the Army of Death was found, where
the carnage had been most fearful, beside that
black Standard of the Wolf which he had de-
fended so fiercely to the last. His Helmet had
fallen from his head; and there, like a tree that
has been charred and blackened by the lightning, he was stretched, grim and ghastly, but
still alive, on a great heap of iron Spears. Beside him lay his gigantic Horse and his battered
Sword. But on that field of doom there were
no mourners to weep over the slain.

There was a conflict between the Hosts of
light and the Hosts of darkness over every
Bride of the King when the River had to be
crossed: but this battle of which I have told
you was the last of all. After this the Desert
and the River passed away.

By the greatness of the strife you may judge
of the pricelessness of the Bride; how the King
loved her; how He wished to have her with
Him in His Home. In the same way you may

judge of the bitter hatred with which the dark
Warriors hated her; and of the fierceness with
which they sought to kill her.

She stood in the twilight by the water-edge,
and the Princes gathered round her.

Now I wish I could tell you how they loved
and pitied her. They were strong and unconquerable; but I can not tell you how tender-
hearted they were. They had won hundreds of
battles against fearful odds; no enemy had ever
seen their backs and no fear had ever touched
their hearts; they had just swept away the
mighty Army of the rebels, as the wind sweeps
away the dust in March : but the tears stood in
their eyes and trickled down their faces, as they
saw the Bride of their King, in her gray Hood
and Cloak, in her innocence and helplessness,
going down through the midst of them into the
icy Stream. Their hearts were full of love and
pity. Very dear to them, for love of the King,
was this Pilgrim who had come to the passage
of the River.

She stept into the Stream. The icy water
sent a trembling through her soul. I heard her
cry out to the King, and her voice sank into my
heart. I started forward to help her, but I

could not get near her. I heard the rushing of
the River, and I knew that the King would
help her, as she said, ' O how fearful this River
is ; I did not think it would be like this. How
darkly the water slides onward. Be with me, O
my Love in this hour. Be with me and help
me, for this River is very cold, and I am
sinking.' The King, who was always close to
her, then spoke to her : and His voice had never
before seemed so full of comfort. He said ;
' Out of the depths I will hear thy voice ; I will
listen to thy prayer, and when thou goest
through the waters they shall not destroy thee.
I, the Holy One of Israel, am thy Saviour. I
will bring thee to thy Home, and thou shalt
lie on My Heart for ever.' Again I heard her
cry out, and her voice was full of pain as she
said to the King ; 'O how piercingly cold this
water is. I can hardly bear it ; my feet are
like ice. O my Love, how quickly it is rising ;
it is gathering round my heart. I am sinking
beneath it, Divine Saviour ; it is closing over
me. O be with me in these depths, and let Thy
Hand hold me. O come nearer to me, Divine
Love ; nearer still ; nearer, Thou Loved One : I
am not yet near enough, not yet close enough,

to Thee. O how fearful this is : merciful Love, how terrible these waters are. O how dark it is ; how cold it is. I am not near enough to Thee. I am in agony. It is going through me. I can not bear it. O come nearer to me, nearer to me, nearer to me, my merciful Saviour.'

Now all this time, the Serpents of the Desert and the Reptiles of the Valley, under other forms, were swimming in the water. They seemed far larger in the gloaming than they really were, and looked like great River-monsters, horrible and fearful. She trembled for a moment ; then all fear passed away. The worst was over.

The waters covered her ancles ; they reached her knees ; they rose to her heart. Then her voice came to me over the flood ; 'O merciful Love, the worst is over. The waters are rising over my head, but I do not fear them now. I feel the touch of Thy Hand, and it makes me strong. O how near to me Thou art, my compassionate Love. I hear a most thrilling melody: I see the light of my Home. I never dreamed how sweet it would be to go beneath the dark water. O light '——

With her Olive-spray in her hand she went

beneath the water as a great light fell on her from the Cedar-crowned Mountain. She saw the brightness of her Home. As the dark water closed over her, her Hood and Cloak were very white and glittering ; and her Olive-branch was very bright. A smile of everlasting gladness shone on her face, as she went beneath the water that she might go to her Love ; that she might find Him in her Home. The water closed over that smile.

A Ripple spread itself out on the swiftly-flowing River.

Her dark Veil floated away down the Stream.

Then the Wind came up with a sorrowful sighing ; and the River made a dirge-like murmuring ; and thus the Wind and the River together sang over her, sweetly, solemnly : and that Song was the Requiem of the Bride.

CHAPTER X.

AMONG THE LILIES.

'O LIGHT of the Face of God!' she said, as she rose from the dark water of the River. White-robed and golden-girdled, she passed, when the Morning Star was shining, with her Olive-branch in her hand, into the Garden of the King. He met her at the Gate. That Gate was made of Pearl, and by it you passed through the Jasper Wall that encircled His City. In His majesty, He came to her in the midst of His Princes. Light fell from Him as He came, and gladness hung around His steps. She looked upon His Face ; her eyes drank in His beauty, and her heart throbbed with the greatness of its love. She gazed upon Him, and could not say a word, but waited to hear Him speak. He said, ' Esther.' Then she said, ' It is the King in His Beauty : my God and my Love.' His Princes then knew her name, but they had not known it before. The King

gave her also another name which was only
known to Him and to herself. With great
reverence they looked on as He stooped down
and kissed her with those Divine Lips that once
had been burnt up with an agony of thirst on
the Cross. She remembered those words, 'I
thirst,' and those other words, 'Let Him kiss
me with the Kiss of His Mouth.' Her Homeward road was ended. She knew now that she
was for ever with the King.

Then she understood all that He had done.
The Lover of her soul was revealed, and she
saw Him with open face. She knew in part no
longer, for she stood before the Uncreated
Light.

Up to this time I have been telling you of
these things for the most part by images which
bring the reality before your minds. Thus the
helps and dangers of our pilgrimage have come
before us : and thus we have thought of the
Home to which the Bride was going. Now she
is in that Home and the Veil is taken away.
So I must speak more plainly, taking much
out of a most Divine Book which many servants
of the King had written. She is now on
Mount Sion, singing the new Song before Him.

K

The Heavenly New Jerusalem is her Home. The King had said that in His Father's House were many Mansions. He also said that He would make ready a place for His Brides that they might be for ever with Him. A servant whom He loved had told this to the Pilgrims in the Desert. Now that she is in His Presence she lifts up her hands to Him and says ; 'This is the rest of which Thou didst tell me : this is the Home that Thou didst promise to make ready for me.' It was the same Divine love that she remembered so well in the Darkness and the Storm : but then it had been in the depth of anguish, whereas now it is in the height of joy. Still it was the same love, deathless and boundless, and without a shadow of change.

His Warriors clustered round Him in the light. Nearest to Him were the seven Princes who had led the most elect Warriors in the great battle on the Plain. Nearest of all were the three mighty Princes in whose Helmets burned the Sapphire and Emerald and Jasper on that day. The Jewels now gleamed with a seven-fold brightness. Every Warrior in the King's Army, standing in the day-light, among

the Lilies, had now a Plume like His. Very
beautiful were their Plumes of white mingled
with red; and very dazzling was the sheen of
their Armour, as it flashed against the sky.
Brightest of all was the sheen of the red and
the silver and the golden Armour of the three.
But she did not see the bright-robed Warriors
nor the glancing of their golden Crowns: she
saw only the Face of the King, full of love for
her; the Face that had looked upon her with
such a Divine pity in the Torrent and the Rain.
A song of angels, entrancing in its strength and
sweetness, rose up from amid the bright-eyed
Flowers in the Garden; rose throbbingly
through the shining air; trembled around her
as she stood among the Lilies: but she did not
hear one note of that thrilling hymn; she heard
only the Voice of the King, sweeter than the
songs of the morning, than the sound of many
waters. He had been with her through the
Valley and the River, though she saw Him not.
Now He has come to her in the light of the
day, among the Lilies and the Pomegranates.
She sees Him and hears His Voice: gazes on
Him without words in the greatness of her love:
and then says to herself, 'I thought that I had

seen Him and heard Him speak in the Desert.
I have never seen Him before; I have never
heard His Voice before.' Thus the King
welcomed her to the many Mansions of His
Father's House. She said to herself, 'I have
never loved Him till now. All the love that
seemed so great is nothing. I have never loved
Him till now.'

As she spoke there rose in her mind the
remembrance of Nazareth and Bethlehem and
Egypt and Thabor and Calvary. She saw the
rock-hewn Sepulchre and the Divine foot-prints
on Olivet. Her dim thoughts about the love
and sorrow of the King were now transfigured
with the beauty of the day. Brighter than all
things else, and sweeter than all things else,
there lay in her heart the splendour of the name
of Jesus.

If you ask me why I am not telling you of
her Home in the same way as I told you of her
pilgrimage, I answer, because all my thoughts
about the Heavenly Kingdom are so poor and
dark, that I must mix them up with the life-
giving thoughts which the King Himself put
into the hearts of His messengers.

His Princes in their strength and beauty

stood round. Love and gladness filled their souls of fire, for now they understood what He did in the old days, when He took off His Crown, and stept down from the Door of His Palace, and went out into the Dark.

Through His sorrow the Bride has now come within the Wall behind which He had been standing while she went through the days of her pilgrimage. She has come up from the Desert, like a pillar of smoke of aromatical Spices, of Myrrh, and of Frankincense. Now she is in the light that fell from the lattices on her way. She is near the golden Throne : and the King wears the Diadem of His Espousals in the day of the gladness of His Heart.

The Morning Star was shining, when He stood with His Bride in the Paradise of Pomegranates, amid the Fruits of the Orchard. His Lilies and all His deathless Flowers were gleaming in the Light. The Cypress Trees and the majestic Cedars lifted their waving branches. The pink bloom of the Almonds sparkled among the milk-white May. The Morning Star shone brightly over that Garden of the King.

At last the Bride lifted up her eyes and saw

all the loveliness of the Garden. I cannot tell you of her thankfulness to her Love for His gifts, and for all the blessedness of her Home. There were no words which could tell of its beauty, and yet it was all as nothing to the great gift that He had given her in Himself.

Round the Garden was a Hedge of May interlaced with Honeysuckle and Jessamine. The scent filled the air, and hung round the City of the King. That Garden seemed to be the Orchard, transfigured and glorified, filled with the wealth of Spring and Summer and Autumn, intermingled and changeless.

The Fountain of Gardens riseth before the Bride with its silvery spray ; and she sees a River of Living Water running with a strong stream from the Well on Libanus. The Vines in flower yield a sweet smell as she looks at the young harts on the Mountains of Bether. She is among the Spikenard and Saffron, the Sweet Cane and Cinnamon. The north wind and the south wind are heavy-laden with the sweetness of that Garden of aromatical Spices. Her garments are fragrant with Myrrh and Stacte and Cassia out of the Ivory Houses. With gladness and rejoicing she is in the Temple of the King.

Hills rose up in that Garden, and the River from Libanus flowed through it. In it, as I will tell you presently, were the Altar and City of the King. The Trees shone in the brightness of the day, and the Birds were singing overhead in their branches. The Thrush and the Black-bird and the Nightingale sang such songs as they had never sung before. The soaring Eagle looked with his undazzled eye on a brighter light than he had ever gazed on before. The Swans on the glassy Streams were far more graceful and far more stately than ever. The Swallows had never before been so beautiful, glancing like gleams of light above the River: and, more musically than ever, the Doves mur-mured among the branches of the Trees, among the Blossom and the Fruit, for the Winter was past, and the Rain was over and gone, and the voice of the Turtle was heard in that land. The air was laden with fragrance, and the River made sweet music as it flowed. On its Banks and on the Hills and all through the Garden the Flowers of the Field were sweet and beautiful. The golden-starred Orange Trees and the Myrtles grew in new loveliness : and the Lilies and Pomegranates were like the brightness of

the Day. But among the Flowers there, the
sacred Passion-Flower was far the most glorious
of all.

There were queenly Roses, many-coloured,
many-scented ; and sceptre-like Lilies, golden-
hearted and stately. There were Kalmias and
Heaths and spear-like Gladioles with their
ruddy bloom. The Lilies of the Valley grew
amid their leaves. Nepenthe was there, and
Asphodel, and deathless Amaranth.

The King stood with His Bride in the Garden
of Pomegranates and Lilies, beneath the Cypresses and Cedars, in the Myrtle-thicket. She
could only say, ' Stay me up with Flowers ;
compass me about with Apples ; for I am fainting with love.' She gazed on His Face and
saw Him in His Beauty. She was conscious
only of Him. She said to Him, ' It never came
into my heart to think what all this loveliness
would be. Now, my Divine Lord, I know what
Thy promises are.' His left Hand was under
her head, and His right Hand embraced her.
She said, ' My God and my Love.'

The Birds were singing in the Trees: the
River murmured along its grassy Banks : all the

Flowers in the Garden poured forth their sweetness and their light.

The Morning Star was shining brightly in the sky, when the King stood with His Bride among the Lilies.

His Princes were round Him in their gleaming beauty. His garments were like snow, and the Hair of His Head like clean wool. His Throne was like flames of fire, and its wheels like a burning flame. From before Him a swift stream of fire went forth. Thousands of thousands of His Princes ministered to Him, and ten thousand times a hundred thousand stood before Him. He was girded with a golden girdle and His Feet were like fine brass in a burning furnace. His Eyes were like a flame of fire: but they were also like Doves upon brooks of water, that are washed with milk and sit by the plentiful streams. His Lips were as Lilies dropping choice myrrh: and His Voice as the sound of many waters. His Princes listened with great reverence as He said; 'Through long and lonely ways, through sorrow and darkness, I have brought thee to thy Home, My Sister and Spouse. Through countless years I have been going down to My Garden to gather Lilies : I

have been going down to that Garden in
mist and snow, in heat and cold. But now I
have brought thee to this Garden where the
Lilies never die. Here thou shalt be with Me
for ever.' She answered; 'O Divine Saviour,
the greatness of Thy love overpowers me.
The beauty of my Home overpowers me too.
Thou art mine. Now I see the glory that no
eye in the darkness hath ever seen : and now I
hear the sounds that no ear in the Desert hath
ever heard. O Jesus, my Loved One, let me lie
in silence a little while on Thy Heart.' After a
while she looked up and said; 'Jesus, my Love,
I am drinking the new Wine with Thee in Thy
Father's Kingdom. For me the banquet is
ever spread. Thou hast made me, Thy disciple,
like my Master; Thou hast made me, Thy
servant, like my Lord. I do not deserve to be a
handmaid in Thy House, and Thou hast made
me Thy Bride. I was a beggar in the streets,
and Thou hast espoused me to Thyself for ever,
and hast brought me to Thy Home. Would
that I could tell Thee about my love; but I
need not; for Thou knowest all things, and
Thou knowest that I love Thee.' 'Many
things,' the King said, 'were dark to thee, while

thou wast wandering in the Desert: but are
they not all plain now, and easy to be understood? Now that Thou understandest it, was
not the Desert a fitting prelude to this? Didst
not thou do wisely to believe in Me and to trust
Me, not following thy own judgments, not being
led away by thy own thoughts?' 'Indeed, my
Love,' the Bride answered, 'I see now how wise
Thou wast in all things and how good. I never
doubted it: I always knew it: but now I see it
and know it clearly.' 'With a great love,' the
King said, 'I loved thee in the land of death.
In My love and in My pity I came to thee
often under the Palms after I had carried thee
through the Torrent. With love and pity, as
thou knowest well, I helped thee through the
Valley and the River. Now, My Sister and
Bride, I love thee with an everlasting love in
this Home of the Redeemed.' 'Incarnate Love,'
she answered, 'Thy Voice is in my ears and in
my heart the sweetest sound that I have ever
heard. It thrills through me. Thou hast told
me of Thy love, without which I must die even
here among the Lilies. Thou hast spoken of
the Darkness and the Torrent: but Thou
hast not said how terrible that darkness was to

Thee: how the Creeping Things made Thee shudder. Thou hast said nothing of the Wind, of the fierceness of the Torrent, of the storm of Rain that beat so pitilessly in Thy Face. Thou hast said nothing of this: but I remember it all, and I will speak of it here, in the midst of Thy radiant Princes. But, O my Lord and my God, everything now is glorified by the light, as once everything was dimmed by sorrow.' The King said; 'Thou hast wounded My Heart, My Sister, My Spouse. I have made thee chains of gold inlaid with silver. Thou art fair, O My love, thou art fair. Thou art fair, My beloved, and beautiful. My beloved, I am thine and thou art Mine, for ever.' To this the Bride answered, 'I sit beneath Thy Shadow Whom I have desired; and the Fruit that Thou givest me is sweet to my taste. O my Loved One, the Winter is past, and the Rain is over and gone. The Fig Trees are covered with fruit, and the Vines in flower yield a sweet smell. I hear the voice of the Turtle, and the Flowers have appeared in the land.' Then the King said; 'My Sister, My Spouse, is a Garden enclosed, a Fountain sealed. Thou art in a Paradise of Pomegranates: and the Fruits of the Orchard

are thine. Spikenard and Cyprus and Saffron
and Sweet Cane and Cinnamon are round thee.
Myrrh and Aloes and all the chief Perfumes
make thy raiment fragrant. The Trees of
Libanus overshadow thee. Thou art with Me
now for ever, in thy Home among the Lilies.'
You could see how these words filled her heart
with joy. Her soul was full of adoration, as
she said ; 'O my Love, I am indeed Thine for
ever : and for ever I lie on Thy Heart. Thou
hast compassed me about with Apples ; Thou
hast stayed me up with Flowers : and I am
fainting with love.' It seemed as if the King took
a delight in speaking of His sufferings, for He
said ; 'I sought for thee in the Desert, and now
thou art with Me for ever in this Garden. I
came to thee beneath the sable Plumes, and now
the Palms are waving over thee for ever. The
blackness of darkness was once thy lot, and
now this Day-spring of My love is for ever thy
Home.' It was always a great gladness to the
Princes when the King spoke of what He had
gone through. The Bride also rejoiced, and
her words were words of thankfulness : 'Divine
King, I never can tell Thee what Thou art to
me : I never can tell Thee of my love. Thou

hast given me all things : Thou hast stayed me
up with Apples. The Pomegranates and the
Lilies are round me. Thou hast compassed me
about with the Flowers of Thy Garden : and I
am fainting with love. No words ever can say
how dear Thou art to me for all Thy sufferings
and for all Thy gifts. Thou hast made me
Thy own for ever. I shall look for ever on the
Crystal River. I shall dwell for ever beneath
the Tree of Life. I am sheltered in Thy abode.
I am for ever in the glory of Thy Face. O how
great is the sweetness, Divine Lord, which Thou
givest to those that fear Thee. How lovely are
Thy Tabernacles, Divine King. My soul and
my flesh rejoice in Thee, the living God. Thy
mercy is great towards me, and Thou hast
saved my life from hell. I will praise Thee,
my God, with my whole heart: and I will
magnify Thy Name for ever.'

Thus she stood among the Lilies with the
King when the scarlet blossoms of the Pomegranates were gleaming in His Garden. It was
the Garden of the Beloved ; and there was the
Fruit of His Apple Trees.

The Morning Star was shining in the sky.
The Hedge of May and Jessamine was very

sweet in the dewy Morning; the Birds sang in the Trees; and the River flowed with a silvery murmur to the Sea.

The mighty Princes were round her: and a flood of gladness swept through her soul, when she knew that she was for ever in her Home. She looked round, and gazed on its beauty. It was as a Rainbow giving light in the bright Clouds, and as the Flower of Roses in the days of the Spring, and as the Lilies that are on the brink of the Waters.

The light lay on the Asphodel and Amaranth. The white bells and green leaves of the Lilies of the Valley among which she stood were shining in the golden thongs of her Sandals, as the stately Lilies, growing round about her, shone in the bright Armour of the Princes.

She looked on the splendour of the City. It seemed like the Orchard transfigured in light. It seemed also like the Desert transfigured and made new. Wonderful as this is, yet so it was. I was told that it was so, because the King had promised that He would make all things new in His Home beyond the River. She looked upon the Valley and the Water-

courses and the Hills, and saw the Flowers
that were growing everywhere, and the Trees
of the Meadow and the Mountain and the
Wood. All the Trees of Libanus were there in
that enclosed Garden. Many were new, such
as she had never seen before ; but many were
the Trees that she had loved in the Desert.
• They were transfigured, indeed, and were made
like those that had never grown out of the
Garden of the King. He had once promised
that He would plant in the wilderness Cedars
and Olive-trees and Myrtles ; and that He would
set in the Desert the Fir-tree, the Elm, and the
Box-tree together.

Drooping Willows grew by the water, but
they did not seem sorrowful there : and the
Aspens were graceful in the day-spring, but
they did not tremble there. The Firs on the
tops of the Mountains lifted their crown-like
branches to the sky. Gray Olives and feathery
Tamarisks and honey-bearing Lindens and
silvery Birches and Mountain-ashes with their
clusters of Berries, like Coral—all these grew in
that wide-spreading Garden of the King.
Besides these there were lofty Elms and stately
Chestnuts and shady Sycamores and acorn-

laden Oaks and majestic Beeches. The day-spring fell upon the Trees, and the River flowed onward to the Sea.

Everywhere, through all that Garden, by Hill and Dale, in the Meadows and the Woods and the Orchards, there was a wealth of Flowers and Fruits in the mingled glory of Spring and Summer and Autumn. Golden Harvests were standing in the fields; the Vineyards were filled with white and purple bunches; the Trees in the Orchards were laden with many-coloured Blossom and Fruit; and all the Flowers of the Year were among them. The Mountain and the Hill praise the King for evermore, and the Trees of the Heavenly country clap their hands. He rejoices in the glory of Libanus. The Vintage there never mourns and the Vines never languish. The Earth bringeth forth its fruit; the Fig-tree and the Vine have yielded their strength. The fruitful Trees and all Cedars praise the Lord.

In the Brooks also that crossed the Garden, hither and thither, filled with water from the River flowing out of a Lake by the Palace of the King, there were many beautiful Flowers. That Lake was the Well on Libanus, beside

L

which the Throne of the King was set. There
the golden-hearted Water-lilies ever shine in
the brightness of the day; and never hide
themselves beneath the water, for no shades of
evening ever fall upon that Land. The Flags
too pierce the air with yellow blossoms and
lance-shaped leaves. There grow the feathery
racemes of the Buckbean, and the white
whorls of the Arrow-head. Water-violets, pale-
lilac, shine above their leaves, for their leaves
are not beneath the surface there. There too
are bright Marsh-marigolds, and there the
Flowering-Rush lifts up its head with its
diadem of rose-coloured bloom.

Beside the Water-courses were Forget-me-
nots, like the blue colour of the Cloak of the
Bride whom the Serpents could not harm; and
pink Willow-herb; and patches of Saxifrage
like golden mats; and Lythrum in its crimson
beauty. There too bloomed clumps of Olean-
ders, some pink and some white, with clusters
of almond-scented Flowers.

On the Plain were Anemones and Celandine
and Cowslips and Cranesbills and sweet Wood-
ruff and Bugloss and Daffodils and Stars of
Bethlehem and lilac-veined Woodsorrel. There

were Stitchworts with star-like blossoms; and
Milkworts, white and purple. The bracts of
the Poinsettias, like scarlet laces, grew amid
the white Christmas-Roses. There too were
Pimpernels and sunny Daisies and Snowdrops;
and Crocuses, like yellow Topaz; and Speed-
well, like Turquoise; and Orchises, like Amethyst; and Hyacinths, like Sapphires; and
Lilies, like Sceptres; and Gladioles, like Spears.
Primroses and Violets mingled their fragrance.
All the sweetness of the Year hung over that
Garden of the King; and all the brightness of
the Year shone in it.

On the Hills gleamed the yellow balls of the
Globe-flower. Mountain-Pansies and Flax and
Foxglove and Grass of Parnassus and Hare-
bells and Eye-bright and Butterworts and
Sundews covered the Hills with beauty. There
bloomed Trientalis and Linnæa and Pyrola
and Mountain Avens with its starry Flowers.
Beside these were our Lady's Mantle, and our
Lady's Slippers, and the white tufts of our
Lady's Cushion. There too were aromatic
Thyme, and Heather, and deep-blue Gentian.
Azaleas and Rhododendrons covered the Hills
with a many-coloured robe. There were clumps

of blue and orange, of red and green, of yellow and violet. Amid them were flashes of white and scarlet; of white and crimson; of white and purple. High above all, the Rock-lily lifted to the sky its crimson crown.

The Bride stood among the Lilies; in the gleaming of white and scarlet Blossoms; in the fragrance of the bright-eyed Flowers; amid the songs of the Birds; beneath the waving of the Trees. All Fruits were there, in the day of the bounty of the King: the old and the new He had kept for her. Very bright were her Sandals, as she looked on the beauty of the Garden; on the radiance of the Altar in the Myrtle-thicket; on the splendour of the Palace, rising up by the River, among the Flowers and many-fruited Trees. She had her Olive-branch in her hand; but, though it was brighter than it had ever been before, you could see no light flowing from it, because of the glory of the Day in which she stood.

Her soul was filled with love, for she saw the King in His beauty.

Then her thoughts went back to the Caverns of Creeping Things and the River that rushed on fiercely to the Sea. She could only look up in the Face of the King and say to Him, 'O Divine Love, the darkness is past for ever : O my Loved One, I am now for ever in this Home with Thee.' All her love rose over her, and bowed her spirit before the King, as she stood with Him in the midst of His Warriors with their Plumes of white and red. Then there shone before her, as she looked, the Altar, jewelled and flower-decked, and beyond it the Home of the King in His City by the Lake. She said to herself, with a thrill of joy : ' How He must have loved me to go down for me into the darkness : how He must have loved me to have made for me this Home of bliss : how He must love me now to wish to have me with Him for ever. He knows how I love Him in return. He knows that I love Him above all things and that to me He is all in all. He sees how I love Him with all my heart and soul and strength.' When she spake thus to herself a flood of joy swept through the very depths of her spirit.

She stood with the King. amid His Princes. Their hearts, strong and tender, throbbed with a great love for her as she looked on His Face ; with a greater love still for the King Himself

Who had brought her through the Desert
and the River. Beautiful and majestic
were those Princes of the King as they
gathered round Him in His Home beyond
the Flood.

She stood with her Love among the Lilies.
The fragrance of the Garden rose up like a
pillar of smoke of Aromatical Spices, of Myrrh
and Frankincense. Trees covered with blossom
and fruit were the answer to the thistles and
nettles of the Desert. The Birds amid the
leaves sang their sweetest songs. ·No words can
tell the splendour of the Princes as they stood
round the King in that fadeless Garden among
the Lilies and Pomegranates.

The deathless Amaranth grew there.

All the blessedness of which He had told her
so often in the Desert was now her inheritance
for ever. The way, weary and dark, was ended.
The road, thorn-strewn, tear-bedewed, had led
her to her Home.

The Morning Star shone brightly over the
Cedars and Palms. A great love filled the
Heart of the King, and flowed down to the.
heart of the Bride. The North wind and the
South wind blew through that Garden of

aromatical spices, and over the Well of Living Waters, while through the Flowers and in the Light the River went down with music to the Sea.

CHAPTER XI.

HIGH among the Lilies and Pomegranates in the Myrtle-thicket, at the foot of the Hill where the Cedar-crown was gently waving in the wind, stood the Altar, gleaming in the light. Thorns and Thistles grew in the Desert: but in the land beyond the Flood, instead of Thorns were Cypresses and Firs, and instead of Nettles were Myrtle-trees. A Man, that is the King, was named for an everlasting sign: and He stood among the Myrtles at the foot of the Hill.

Though there was no sun there, yet the refreshing light was far brighter than the rays that fell so fiercely on the head of the Bride, as she went Homeward through the Desert. The brightness of that light fell on the Altar, and the sweetness of the Flowers hung round it. Beyond it, on the banks of the Lake from which the River was flowing, were the Palace and City of the King. In His Palace was His golden Throne with silver pillars. All the path, as you went up to it, was covered with purple. When His Bride first stood with Him among the Lilies she saw this Altar. Then it seemed wondrous; but now it was as if the glory of seven days were shining upon it; as if the fragrance of seven gardens were clinging around it. It stood in its majesty amid the brightness of the Flowers. The white-tufted Myrtles grew near it. A little way beyond, higher up the Hill and covering it to the top, were the Cypresses and Palms and Cedars. At last she had come to Libanus and the waving of its Diadem of green.

High among the Lilies and Pomegranates stood the Altar of which the King had so often told her in the Desert; of which He had spoken to her plainly under the Palms, more plainly still under the Apple Tree in the Orchard, and most plainly under the little Palm-cluster that grew in it near the Hedge. For hours, days, years, she had thought about this Altar, and wondered what it would be like, and fashioned it to herself in her heart, amid the darkness. Through the years, heavy-footed, heavy-winged, she had loved it unseen, for she knew

that there the King, her Lord and her God,
would make her His Own for ever. Even in
the Desert, so long as she was faithful, she was
His Sister and Bride; but before the Altar she
would be His Sister and Bride for ever; dwelling with Him in the Home from which she
goeth out no more. I have already told you of
her suffering in the wilderness; of the anguish
of heart that blinded her often and crushed her:
of the agony that burned like fire in her soul,
creeping into the depths of her spirit. Through
all her sorrow, and through all the loneliness of
her waiting the thought of this Altar had been
her rest and her stay, a hope so blessed that
she could only think of it with tears. Under
the Palm Trees this thought came to her in
its freshness; in the Shadow of the Rock it
sheltered her from the heat. It heartened her
as she walked among the fiery Serpents; as
she went down through the Valley; as she
passed on in the darkness amid the Reptiles; as
she stept into the River like ice. It filled her
heart with joy as she went into the Orchard;
as she passed through the Gate into the Garden
of the King; as she stood among the Lilies,
when the Morning Star was shining. She often

spoke thus to herself : 'The way is very long ; the anguish is very great. What can I do ? How can I bear it ? How can I go on ? A great sorrow fills my spirit : my heart within me is sinking. What am I to do ?' Then at once she said, turning to the King's promise, ' Divine Love, what will it all matter one day ? What will it matter, when the night and the road are ended ? What shall I care for all this pain when I come to be with Thee for ever in Thy City built without hands? Before the Altar Thou wilt make me Thy own for ever.' Whenever she said this, even in her woe, tears of gladness trickled down her cheeks. This hope had been ever with her : and so she had thought unceasingly of that Altar, and wondered what its beauty would be, and fashioned it for herself in her heart. Now at last she is standing before it and sees it; and it is far beyond all that she had thought. The Princes smile and give praise to the King, when they see her gladness and her wonder. They love her with a great love as she stands in her graciousness before the Altar. Her golden hair falls round her like a glory, and her raiment is white and glittering, so as no fuller on earth could make white. She has a Girdle of Gold, studded with Jasper and Pearl. As she stands there the King has hold of her hand.

Thus she gazed on the Altar of which she had thought so much in the Desert, and she was lost in wonder at its beauty. She spoke of it to the Prince, who had always watched over her on her way, and they rejoiced together with a very great joy. He was standing near her and was close to the King. But her greatest gladness was the thought that she owed all her blessedness to the King and to Him alone. Whatever help she had had from His Bride, untouched by the Serpents, and from His Princes, had all come from Him.

I must try to tell you what that Altar was like: but though I remember it well, and sometimes think that I can see it even now, I feel that what I can say will only put into your minds a faint shadow of its brightness.

The Altar was an Opal: and on it were tokens of the past. In the centre, on the front, was a Palm Tree by a Fountain of Water, and round it was a circle of Emeralds and Pearls. Each Pearl was the size of a sparrow's egg, and was set in seven leaves of Emerald. The sacred

Passion-flower and the Pasque-flower and the Alleluia-flower were twined together. On the right of this was a band of Sapphires round a Sheaf of Corn : and on the other side in a ring of Chrysolites was a Vine with green and purple bunches. The Tabernacle was a Sardonyx, red and white : and it was for an everlasting token of what had been in the Desert. For this reason, though it was needed not, the King kept it there. The Candlesticks and Vases were of pure gold set with Pearls and Amethysts. These Pearls were about half the size of those in the front of the Altar. In the Vases were white Asters, and scarlet Gladioles, and behind them were Fronds of Fern. The Steps of the Altar were of Beryl, and the Pavement of Topaz and Chalcedony and Jacinth.

Behind the Altar, in the centre, grew an Apple Tree laden with Fruit ; and among the Apples were Blossoms of rose-pink and white. On one side of the Apple Tree was a Hawthorn covered with milk-white Bloom ; and on the other side was a Pomegranate gleaming with scarlet Flowers. At each end of the Altar was an Almond Tree brightened with pink blossom; and a little way from each was a Myrtle.

Round the Almond Trees grew white Roses
and golden Lilies ; but round the Myrtles
the Roses were crimson and the Lilies white.
These two Myrtles were larger and sweeter than
those that grew in the Myrtle-grove.   In all
the beds of the Garden, whatever other Flowers
there might be, there were always Lilies and
scarlet Pomegranates.

Upon the Altar fell a light like the sunshine
of June for brightness.   It was not, however,
like the sunshine in the Desert, but was refreshing as a breeze that cometh up from the sea.
Overshadowing all were the Cedars and Palms :
and through their gently-waving branches that
light fell on the Apple Tree and the Pomegranates and the Myrtles.   Then it streamed
down in sparkling rivulets on the Altar.   The
Precious Stones were all bright with the brightness of the Day.

Thus that Altar stood among the Myrtles in
the Land that was dwelt in and at rest.   All
the Princes heard the King. speak good words
and comfortable words.   They saw how he had
gone back to His Own Land in mercies :   how
in it His everlasting House had been built.
Their Armour and golden Helmets and Spears

flashed back again the brightness of the day. Some of them had branches of Olive in their hands, or branches of Myrtle or branches of Palm : some had Lilies, and some had Harps, and some had still their silver Spears. But I saw only one Sword ; all the rest were in their Scabbards. The mighty Prince, with the Sapphire in his Helmet, was leaning on the hilt of the great Sword with which he had struck down the red-plumed Leader in the midst of the Rebels. They who still had their silver Spears before the Altar were the Princes who had guarded the Bride as she went down from the Valley to the River. Never had the Jewels in the Helmets of the Seven burned with such a light as now.

Standing before the Altar, in her purity and graciousness, she had in her left hand her Olive-spray. But now it looked like a Sceptre.

As the King, with His many Crowns, in His royal Apparel, stood there with His Bride, He had hold of her hand. His Heart was full of an everlasting love.

The Morning Star had faded before the brightness of the Day, when the King stood in the Myrtle-thicket.

In the midst of His Princes He said; 'Thou hast come to Me as the Morning, fair as the Moon, bright as the Sun. Thou hast wounded My Heart, My Sister, My Spouse; Thou hast wounded My Heart. I have set thee as a Seal on My Arm, for My love is stronger than death.'

The redeemed Bride answered Him; 'O Divine Spouse, my soul melts at the sound of Thy Voice; and my heart grows faint with love when Thou art speaking. My Loved One, my Saviour, it is the same Voice, that I heard beyond the River. It is the well-remembered Voice that sank into the depths of my soul, when the waters of the Torrent went rushing and leaping past Thee and the Rain was driven in Thy Face by the Wind. O my Love, even here among these Lilies, before this Altar, every tone of Thy Voice brings back to me a memory of the old days; the old days, my crucified Love, of darkness and sorrow. There are eternal memories of sorrow and of joy; but here the sorrow is gone, and only the joy abideth.' The Princes listened very reverently as the King answered; 'When I saw thee on the top of Amana I loved thee: and when thou didst dwell on Sanir and Hermon I had espoused thee to Myself. I walked on the mountains of the leopards that I might find thee: and I went down into the dens of the lions that I might save thee; that I might bring thee to Myself; that I might keep thee for ever in this Home. Thou hast wounded My Heart, My Sister, My Spouse.' 'Once, Divine Lover of my soul,' she said, 'I sought for Thee, and found Thee not: but now I have found Thee for ever. Now I shall never go away from Thee any more. Once I wandered about the streets and the broadways, about the fields and lanes, seeking for Thee, and I could not find Thee. I cried out aloud and said, 'O my Beloved, art Thou near to me? How long must I be drenched with my sorrow? When shall I see Thee?' I cried out to Thee, and the voice of my anguish pierced the air; pierced the sunshine, or the rack of the tempest, or the tingling darkness of the night: but no answer came. The birds that were singing in the hedges could not tell me about Thee: and the roes and the harts of the field could not bring me to Thee. I sat helplessly, alone in my great anguish, on a heap of stones, in the storm of rain, in the dark night, in the howling of the wind. I said to myself,

M

'I must go on seeking for Him Whom my soul
loveth until I find Him.' I asked the watchmen
of the City if they had seen Thee : but they
had seen Thee not. They thought that I was
beside myself, out of my mind : and I was
beside myself, Thou Lover of my soul ; but not
as they thought. I was out of my mind with
love. I sought for Thee, day and night, through
my exile : but now I have found Thee. Now I
hold Thy Hand before Thy Altar. Now I
shall never go away from Thee again.' A great
thrill went through all the Princes, whenever
the King spoke. So it was now, as He said ;
'My love, thou hast come to Me as the
Morning-rising, fair as the Moon, bright as the
Sun. O Prince's Daughter, thy steps are
beautiful in Shoes among these Lilies. Thy
voice is sweet in My Ears. Thou hast wounded
My Heart, My Sister, My Spouse. Thou art
with Me for ever. I have set thee for ever as a
Seal on My Heart, for My love is stronger than
death.' As He said this, the Lilies seemed to be
sweeter than ever. The Bride looked up to
Him, and clasped her hands, as she said ; 'O
Divine Love, what a giver Thou art. .Thou
didst make me in the Desert very great and

precious promises : but Thou hast given me far
more than I ever hoped. It was not little for
which I looked, Thou Loved One : indeed it
was very much : but Thou art ten thousand
times more. I thought I knew what Thy love
would be, but I did not know it in the least.
Thou art Thyself the Crown of all Gladness ; but
even Thy gifts are more than ever came into
my mind. All things, new and old, Thou hast
kept for me : and I am for ever Thy Own.'

Just then the South wind stirred the leaves of
the Myrtles. The King answered her in these
words ; 'Thy lips, My Spouse, are a dropping
Honeycomb. Honey and Milk are under thy
tongue : and the smell of thy raiment is as the
smell of Frankincense. My Sister, My Spouse,
is a Garden enclosed and a Fountain sealed.
Thy plants are a Paradise of Pomegranates
with the Fruits of the Orchard.' As He spoke
the fragrance of the Lilies rose up round me ;
and His Voice was sweeter than the sound of
many waters. Still with clasped hands, she
answered ; 'Divine Spouse, I can feel Thy love
flowing through my spirit. It is the stream of
pleasure that makes glad the City of the Blest.
But even in the sweetness of this Garden ; even

before this Altar; I can think of nothing, I can know nothing, my Jesus, save that I am with Thee. Thou art all lovely, and chosen out of thousands.' Now it seemed to me as if a splendour ran along the ground and lighted up the Cedars, as this answer of the King fell on my ears; 'With a great love I have espoused thee to Myself. In a great blessedness I have set thee. With a great gladness I rejoice over thee for ever.'

From the Altar she went to her Throne in the City of the King. As she passed through the Garden all its sweetness hung round her, but she herself was far sweeter than all the Flowers that were there. The King took her to His Home, and set her on her ivory Throne.

To every Bride of the King, who went into the Garden of Lilies and came to the Altar, a Throne was given. There was one Throne far brighter than all the rest, such a wondrous Throne of light and beauty that the Princes even could not fully understand it. That was the Throne of the Bride who had never been beyond the fierce River. The other Brides were clothed in white raiment and had Diadems of Gold and Emerald; but this Bride was clothed with the Sun and had twelve Stars in her peerless Crown.

The other Brides, like the Princes, had in their
hands Myrtles or Palms or Olives or Harps or
Lilies : but she, nearest to the King and dearest
to Him, was the Queen, and had in her hand a
silver Sceptre, entwined with Gold, and studded
with Emeralds and Pearls.

That Home of the King in His Paradise was
a very wonder of beauty. It rose up in His
City by the River, beyond the Altar and the
Myrtle-thicket. From the Altar indeed you
saw it very plainly. Above it was the Hill
crowned with Cedars and Palms. Beside it was
the Lake. The Light lay upon it, and the
Flowers grew about it, and the Birds sang round
it, and Creepers hung in masses from its walls,
and stately Trees were near it. Round the
Door grew a Vine laden with grapes ; and
clustering at the Windows were Traveller's-joy,
and the white flowers of the Bindweed, and
Jessamine far sweeter than that in the Hedge of
the Garden. There were Cyclamens, Alkanet,
Columbine, and May-lilies. There shone the
leaves of our Lady's Vine. Close to the walls
of that Palace were Laburnums with their
golden chains ; and all round there was a wealth
of Cluster-Roses. Myrtles grew there like those

round the Altar. There were Bird-cherries, and
Hazels, and White-beam ; and there, too, the
Magnolias loaded the air with sweetness.

The flower-girt Lake on Libanus sparkled in
the light; the Garden was filled with myriad-
starred loveliness : and through the City the
River went down in brightness to the Sea.

This was the Home that the King had pre-
pared for His Bride ; and it shone like Jasper
and Chrysolite and Amethyst through the leaves
and Flowers. In the light rose the golden
Roofs and Pinnacles of the many Mansions
which He had made ready in His City. All
that City was His Home. He had built it
without hands and it was eternal in Heaven.
It had strong foundations, because of the Divine
love by which it had been built. There
sparkled the waters of the Lake and the ever-
flowing River. Down to the edge of the water
grew the Flowers in their fragrance and their
loveliness. All through that City, among the
Beryls and Topazes and Jacinths, hung sweet
clusters of Grapes and Woodbine and Roses.

Now remember that the blessedness of this
Bride was very little to the blessedness of that
other Bride who was never beneath the sable

Plumes; and who saw no river-monsters when she went through the water to the Garden of the King. She had emerald-studded Sandals even in the Desert. But the Bride, of whom I have been telling you, went barefooted along that road, as I said a little while ago; and even among the Lilies, even before the Altar, there was not a Jewel in her Sandals. Whatever the King did for her, whatever He gave to her, He did a myriad times more for the Bride whom the Serpents could not touch : and to her. He gave a myriad times greater gifts, in the light of her Espousals and the blessedness of her Home. But I cannot of course tell you about her now.· I only want you to remember the gladness that filled her heart when she saw the King standing before the Altar, with His ransomed Love, her little Sister. The Home of this Bride, whom no Serpents ever came near, was the most glorious of all that He had given to any whom He had espoused to Himself, lifting them with His strong Hands from the River to the Garden of Lilies.

As I looked it all seemed to come before me in another way. So boundless were the love and wisdom of the King that no one could ever

understand all His beauty or see it all at once.
Suddenly four Living Creatures came like flashes
of lightning. Over the King hung a fiery cloud
with a blaze of Amber. Then there came
Wheels as the appearance of the sea, and above
the heads of the Princes the Firmament was as
crystal. The four Living Creatures before the
King were like lamps and like burning coals
of fire. He sat on a Throne of Sapphire, and
there was a mingled glory of Fire and Amber
within the Throne and round about. The Divine
Man reigned in His glory, and His Voice was
the Voice of the most High God.

Then I fell on my face and adored Him Who
sat on the Throne, and Who liveth for ever and
ever.

Again I looked and saw the Paradise of our
Love as He has told us of it in His Book,
where He says that He is the Flower of the
Field and the Lily of the Valley.

Before me stood His everlasting Home in its
wealth of sweet-scented Flowers by the River as
it flowed from the Well on Libanus. It was a
City of Palaces, bright and strong. The Bride
had gone from the Altar to her Home among the
Lilies and Pomegranates of the Paradise of God.

The Corn stood in the Vineyards with the deathless Vines.

The young Roes and the Harts were on the Hills of aromatical Spices; they were feeding among the Lilies on Hermon and Libanus.

The Garden of Nuts was on Carmel amid the Myrtles and Olives.

One cliff went sheer down into the night. There lay the dim Vale of Kedron ; and, far lower still, amid the blackness of darkness, was Topheth in the Valley of Ennom.

But the Lake was a sea of light : brightness fell upon the Flowers : and through them the Home of the King, high and lifted up, shone in its starry beauty.

The Cypresses and Palms were a Diadem on the heads of the Mountains. In the South wind they made a rustling that mingled itself with the music of the River : and a great light fell on the waving of the branches in the dark-green Cedar-crown.

CHAPTER XII.

A BRIDE of the Crucified King sits throned in the Light, amid the blossom of the Almonds ; amid the Apple Trees, fragrant and golden-fruited and full of bloom ; beneath the dark-green Crown of Cypresses and Cedars ; beneath the waving of the eternal Palms.

Crowned in her Home she sees the Face of the King in His beauty. She is with Him in the Light for ever. Seeing Him as He is, she loves Him with a deathless love, for all that He is in Himself, for all that He has done, for all that He has given her. His Face, once hidden and despised, is now the Light of His City. It is the comfort of His people. She is clothed with the garment of Salvation and covered with the robe of Justice. She is decked with a Crown and adorned with Jewels. Her Just One has come forth as brightness : her Saviour is lighted as a lamp. All the pilgrims see that

Just One, and the Kings see that Glorious One.
She is called by a new name which the Mouth
of the Lord hath named; and is a Crown of
Glory in His Hand, and a royal Diadem in the
Hand of God. She rejoices in the Home that
has been made ready for her, rejoices in the
great gladness of her life: but her true Home
is the love of the King. It is all the more
blessed because she remembers so well the rushing of the Torrent and the drifting of the Rain.
In the peacefulness of her rest, she ever turns
to the Holy One with deeper thankfulness when
she remembers the Serpents, and the Bundle of
Myrrh, and the River in the dark Valley. Even
in the light of her Home she is always calling
to mind the pity of the King that once was hers
in the old time, when He stept down from the
Door of His Home, and went out into the
Storm. Then He sought for her in her sorrow,
amid the ashes of Death, and brought her to
the shelter of His Heart. But now He has no
pity for her any more, but only a measureless
love. He looks on her with His Divine Eyes,
once blinded with blood and tears. But they
are never dimmed now, for God hath wiped
away tears from all faces. Her eyes too are

always bright, for she looks upon His glory. She is like Him, for she sees Him as He is. She says, 'My Beloved is mine and I am His.' She says to Him, 'Thou hast sought for me in the Darkness and in the anger of the Storm by night; Thou hast been with me in the Desert and the Valley; Thou hast brought me to Thyself. I am with Thee for ever now. O my Divine Love, at last I am on Libanus with Thee.' Again she says; 'My Beloved is mine, and I am His. He has brought me to the Lilies. I am with Him in the Light.'

The Lilies and the Pomegranates are gleaming there. A wealth of fragrance and of beauty is stored up in the Garden of the King. But His redeemed Spouse is far sweeter than the Lilies, and far more beautiful than the scarlet Blossoms. His Princes stand round her: and their Spears and Helmets burn in the splendour of the Light. It is like the throbbing of a great sea of fire: but she is far brighter than the gleam of the golden Helmets and the glint of the silver Spears.

But what shall I say of the love with which the King loves her? or of the gladness of heart with which He looks upon her for ever on His

Throne, in the Light of His Kingdom? There
are no words that I know of, which can in the
very least tell of that love. It is altogether
beyond such words as mine, because it is
altogether beyond my thoughts. In a little
way you may understand what it is by calling to
mind all that He went through for her sake;
all the piercingness of pain that He suffered in
the midnight of His sorrow that He might
bring her from the outer darkness to the shelter
of His Home.

In His love He espoused her to Himself;
went to her in the Darkness; gave her comfort
and strength; and at last brought her to the
Lilies. He had pitied her with a great pity in
the time of her suffering. In all her affliction
He was her Saviour. His Princes did not save
her, but He saved her Himself. She seemed
dearer to Him than ever when He thought of
the anguish of her soul. A great tenderness
came over Him when He saw her in her woe.
When He was saving her it never came into
His mind that she had brought the misery on
herself. He loved her; and for her sake went
down into the darkness. Along with His everlasting love there was in His Heart a boundless

pity. Now she needs His pity no more. All that she needs is His love : and that He gives to her in its fulness, without measure. She is with Him for ever in the Light ; and is set for ever as a Seal on His Heart. Once her anguish rose over her like the waters of a flood; now there cometh the flood of her gladness and her peace. Nothing can ruffle the blissfulness of that rest ; nothing can dim the brightness of that joy, in the land beyond the River of Doom. All things are made new. The sun does not fall on her, nor any more heat. She dwells for ever beside the Fountain of Living Waters. Night is no more, and she needs no more the light of the lamp or the light of the sun. Death is no more, nor sorrow, nor mourning, nor crying, nor any kind of pain. The King loves her with a love changeless as Himself; and her heart is always full of an undying love for Him.

His Princes stand round the Throne of ivory and gold. A great gladness thrills through those mighty Spirits when they see how their King rejoices over His Bride, and how He loves His redeemed one with a love that lights up all His City. The ivory Throne stands full in the gleaming of that Light. The River, ever flowing from the Lake, is bright as Crystal.

All the Cedars and Cypresses glisten in the Day-spring. The Almonds flourish; the Vines yield their sweet smell; the Fig Tree puts forth her fruit. The May is very white, and the Apple Trees are bowed down with their load. The Palms overshadow the Fountain; and the water makes a sweet murmuring for ever. But no Desert is round the Palm Trees there; and the King is seen face to face.

The Day, to which no darkness cometh, fills and encircles the City with its Light. The Palace of the King ever shineth in its beauty through the Flowers that hang on its walls; and His Garden always has a sweetness far beyond that of Myrrh and Stacte and Cassia. The King is silent in the greatness of His love. The Jasper gleams in that Home of the everlasting age among the Lilies and Pomegranates. The pure gold of the Streets of the City is like glass. The Gates of pearl are ever open by day; and there is no night there.

I rejoiced greatly when I remembered that the Pilgrim was in the Home from which she would go out no more for ever.

I ask you to bless and thank the King for bringing so many Pilgrims to the shelter of the Paradise of God.

Pray earnestly also that He may bring you, in His great love, to that Home where you may walk with Him for ever in white.

The seven Princes listened very reverently, and their burning Crowns shone more brightly than ever as the King said; 'The waiting has been long, but now the joy is great. I have brought thee to Libanus : I have espoused thee to Myself. Now thou art with Me in the Light; and art crowned in thy Home. All that I have is thine.' The seven Princes again listened with new joy, when the Bride answered Him ; 'O Divine Love, the waiting has indeed been long and fearful. But it is over now; and I have forgotten its pain. What a joy fills my heart when I think that the sorrow and darkness are gone for ever. Through the dim years I kept myself for Thee. They lingered and seemed as if they would never go : but Thou didst give me grace to wait. Thy love fell on the anguish of my heart : Thy comforts refreshed my soul : Thy Hand held me up and led me on my way. Divine Love, the hope of this reward was my only stay. But for this I could not have borne my grief. It was the one thought that saved me from despair, and kept my heart from breaking. But, Thou Loved One, the pain is over now : the sorrow is gone now. I have passed the Valley, and crossed the River, and have come to Thee. Now the darkness cometh to me no more for ever.'

The Warriors listened, and were filled with joy and reverence, as the King spoke to her thus; ' With an everlasting love do I love thee. In the Light I have set thee for ever as a Seal on My Heart. My love is stronger than death.' These words of the King filled her heart with more gladness, and she said ; ' O my Love, I am lost in the greatness of my joy. To me all things are made new. Once the years went over me in my sorrow. Let me speak to Thee of it, my God, in this Light, in this great blessedness, for it makes all my bliss the greater. Once the years went over me and found me in darkness and sorrow. They came and they went : but no joy came near me in the dimness of the way: save only when some Desert-space was past, and I came to Thee under a Palm Tree by a Fountain of Water :

N

or when the Shadow of the great Rock fell on
me and saved me from the heat. Let me talk
to Thee about it now, my Saviour, in this
blessedness ; for it makes my happiness all the
greater. Then no joy came to me in the
banishment of the tents of Kedar ; save when
Thy light fell on me through the gloom. My
Divine Spouse, I love to think of this, and tell
Thee of it now, for it makes me understand
better what I have. Now I am lost in the greatness of my joy. I never loved Thee till now.
The love that I thought so great was nothing.
Even then that love was beyond all other love :
but it was nothing to this. But all that I have
is Thy gift, Thou most bountiful Giver. Now
the eternal years go over me in the fulness of
my bliss. I give Thee all my love, all my
heart, all my soul. Thou art my Divine King
and my God : and I am Thy Sister and Bride
for ever. Thou hast comforted me, and hast had
mercy on Thy poor one. Then my sighs were
many and my heart was sorrowful. I girded
myself with hair-cloth and sprinkled dust on
my head. The tears ran down my cheeks, day
and night : and my heart cried to Thee. My
soul was far away from peace ; and sometimes I

forgot good things. I remember the wormwood and the gall. The Crown fell from my
head, and my joy ceased, and my eyes were
dim. But Thou art good to them that hope in
Thee, and to the soul that seeketh Thee.
Every morning Thy mercies are new : Thy
faithfulness is great. I was lonely, but I
waited for Thee; waited in silence for Thy
Salvation. Now Thou hast brought me out
of darkness into light. Thou hast heard my
voice. Thou hast lifted me up from the lowest
pit; from the waters that flowed over my head.
I am Thy servant, and Thou hast lifted me up;
and I see eye to eye.' Through the splendour
of the Princes came the words of the King;
'Winter is now past: the Rain is over and
gone : the Flowers have appeared in our Land.
The voice of the Turtle is heard in our Land.
Thou hast wounded My Heart, My Sister, My
Spouse. I am the Lord Thy Redeemer.'

Looking upon the Home that the King had
made ready with His Divine Hands, she
answered; 'O, Incarnate Love, all things, new
and old, Thou hast kept for me: all things, new
and old, Thou hast given me here. Thou hast
made me Thy Bride and Sister for ever; I

know nothing, Divine Spouse, save that Thou art perfect and that Thy ways are just and true.'

'Oftentimes,' she went on saying, 'a vision of all this gladness rose up before me in the Desert. Oftentimes a prelude of this filled my heart in the lonely road. Then I was away from Thee, but now I never can be away from Thee again. Often in that sorrow there came a glimmer of this blessedness; and often the brightness shone upon me in a passing gleam: then in a moment the light was lost in the shapeless dark. Now it has come to me for ever: and I see it with my eyes, and feel it in my heart. Tears can never again roll down my cheeks: mourning has fled away for ever: death can come to me now no more. Thou hast given me this white Raiment of my Espousals instead of the sackcloth that covered me beneath the Plumes of Death. Once the Storm-wind swept over me, and the fierce River rushed past me ; and now a gentle Wind makes a rustling among the branches of the Cedars, and this River, like crystal, goes down through the Flowers to the Sea, and makes music in my heart as it goes. Once the darkness over-

shadowed me ; now the great happiness thrills
· through my spirit, and the eternal Light makes
me glad. From the Land of Death Thou hast
brought me to the Land of Life. For a little
while Thou didst forsake me ; but with great
mercy Thou hast gathered me. In a moment
of indignation Thou didst hide Thy Face from
me ; but with everlasting kindness Thou hast
had mercy upon me, for Thou art the Lord,
my Redeemer.' The King then said ; 'O little
one, once tossed with tempest, once without
comfort, I have laid Thy Foundations with
Sapphires, and made thy Bulwarks of Jasper
and thy Gates of Graven Stone.' Again He
said ; 'Thou art all fair, My love, and there is
not a spot in thee. I have given thee rest,
and filled thy soul with brightness, and made
it like a watered Garden, whose Waters cannot
fail.' Then once more He said ; 'All things
new and old, My beloved, I have kept for thee.
Thou art to Me a cluster of Cypress in these Vineyards. In our Gates are all Fruits. Thou art a
Seal upon My Arm, and a Seal upon My Heart.'

Then the Princes who had watched over the
Bride on her Homeward way gave thanks to
the King, and the Voice of their praise went up

like the voice of a great water-flood, round the Ivory Throne.

The sound of that praise was like the noise of a great multitude, like the noise of an army, like the voice of great thunders, like the sound of the Cherubim when they let down their wings.

Then comes the silence of the everlasting love, and it thrills through the Garden of the King. His Bride is white-robed and golden-girdled in the beauty of His Home and the place where His Glory dwelleth. The touch of that Hand, which once held the Staff in the rage of the Torrent, brings upon her as it were a river of peace. His Voice, far sweeter than the sound of many waters, sinks into her heart. It is a voice from the City, a voice from the Temple, a voice from the Throne. As I knelt down and listened, the King spoke seven times. Every time that He spoke, there came, after His words, a silence. He had seven Stars in His right hand, and stood in the midst of seven Golden Candlesticks. All that have ears can hear His words if they choose. This is what He said :

'Thou hast overcome, and I have given thee

to eat of the Tree of Life which is in the Paradise of my God.'

Then came the silence.

'Thou hast been faithful unto death, and I have given thee a Crown of Life.'

Then came the silence.

'Thou hast overcome, and I have given thee the hidden Manna, and the new Name which no one but thyself can know.'

Then came the silence.

'Thou hast overcome, and I have given thee the Morning Star.'

Then came the silence.

'Thou hast overcome, and I have confessed thee before My Father, and before His Angels.'

Then came the silence.

'Thou hast overcome, and I have made thee a pillar in the Temple of My God, and thou shalt go out no more. I have written upon thee the name of My God, and the name of the City of My God, the New Jerusalem; and I have written upon thee My new Name.'

Then came the silence.

'Thou hast overcome, and I have given thee to sit with Me on My Throne, as I overcame and am set down with My Father on His Throne.'

Then again came the great silence in Heaven, as it were, for half-an-hour.

All this while the redeemed Bride gazes, in rapture, on the Face of Jesus in His Kingdom, and drinks in His might and wisdom and tenderness, and knows that she is with Him, loving and loved, for ever. A great gladness overshadows her and fills her heart. The Holy One there is as a flame, and His light is as a fire. She praises the Lord, and calls upon His name. She sings to Him, for He hath done great things; and she rejoices for evermore in the Home that has been built on Sion. The Throne has been made ready in mercy; and One sitteth upon it for ever in truth.

The fragrance of the Fruit, of the Blossom, of the Flowers, hangs over that Garden in the Day which endeth not and in the light which changeth not. The Flowers shine, some like stars, and some like fire-flies, and some like precious stones. The Lilies pour forth floods of sweetness, and the Pomegranates pour forth floods of light. The Cedars wave their branches gently when the South wind cometh. The pink Blossom of the Almond Trees sparkles among them. Beneath them the King walketh in the

light. He hath made known His salvation :
He hath revealed His justice : He hath remembered His mercy. The River claps its
hands and all the Mountains are glad in His
presence. Praise and beauty are before Him :
there is a joyful sound of hymns ; holiness and
majesty are in the sanctuary of His Home for
ever.

Then the ransomed Bride talks with the
Princes about the darkness of the Desert. It
seems as if the blessedness of her Home were
greater through thoughts of the homeless
Wilderness. She remembers the great agony
that once was, but now has passed away for
ever. She calls to mind the anguish of soul
through which the road lay that led up to this
Home among the Lilies. As the River flows
through the Garden, lit up with countless
gleams, she listens to the sweetness of its
murmuring ; and thinks of the Torrent with its
wind-shaken waters and crimson waves. The
Light falls upon her, and she thinks of the Rain
in the darkness of the Night. She looks on the
beauty of the Garden, and while she thanks
Jesus for it there rises before her in memory
the gloom of the Valley through which she

passed. All such thoughts as these make her Home more blessed.

Then, even in that Home of light, she remembers that she has nothing, save those things which the King has given her : and she is gladdened by the thought. Great indeed is her joy to think that all that she is, and all that she has, are His; that all her treasures, whatever they may be, are His gifts ; and that He Himself, her crowned and sceptred Love, is far more than all. He is a Garland of Joy and a Crown of Glory : her only rest, her only reward; and everything else is as nothing. This too makes that Home brighter and more blessed.

The silence of that love thrills through the City of the King. It hangs round the Ivory Throne. The Bridegroom rejoices over the Bride.

She understands the love of the King, and enjoys it for ever. Gazing upon Him in her great love, her love now eternal as His own, she says to herself in her heart, ' He is mine for ever, and I am His for ever' : and she is blest. Once in the Dark, beside the fierce River, her prayer was, ' Come to me, Divine Love, in this unutterable woe :' but now in the Light she says to Him,

'Thou hast brought me to Thyself, and I am with Thee for ever in this unspeakable joy.' Once she lifted up her hands to Him through the darkness; lifted up her clasped hands to Him through the darkness and the storm ; but now, in the Light, she is set for ever as a Seal on His Arm. Once she had ever been·sighing out a De Profundis to Him, Who in His great love had given her a burden of life-long suffering. Then she had felt bowed down with the weight of years as she went through the Desert to her Home. But now she is in that Home for ever, dwelling before the King in wealthy rest. Now in her changeless Youth, and the glory of the Day, she is singing in her heart a ceaseless Te Deum to Him, Who, having brought her in His Own good time from the sorrow in which He set her, has given her such a height of bliss.

There is singing in the Vineyard of pure Wine : and the dew is the dew of the Light. The King reigns in justice, and the Princes rule in judgment. The work of justice is peace, and the service of justice quietness and security for ever. The land has budded forth and blossomed, and flourishes like the lily. It rejoices with joy and praise. The glory of Libanus is given to it;

and there is the beauty of Carmel and Saron.
The acceptable time has come ; and the day of
salvation has been revealed.　Joy and gladness
are found there : there are thanksgiving and the
voice of praise.　The Fir Tree, and the Box Tree,
and the Pine Tree brighten the King's Sanctuary
and make the place of His Feet glorious.　Gold
and Frankincense from Saba are offered on the
rock-built Altar in the House of His Majesty.
He is an Everlasting Light ; the glory of the
Sun that goeth down no more.

He has gone back to that bright Home from
which He stept down, when He went out into
the Dark.　His ransomed One also has past
from the Land of Death through the Desert
and the River.　Her golden Sandals shine
among the Lilies, and the Emeralds in her
Crown burn with a seven-fold gleam.　The
Bundle of Myrrh is now a Cluster of Cypress for
ever.　The Eternal Palms are waving ; the
Cypresses lift up their heads amid the Almond
Trees and the Myrtles ; and a great light of
glory falls on the Branches in the gleaming
Cedar-crown.　The River flows on through the
shining City, and for ever makes it glad.　The
King has brought His Bride from the Dark to

the splendour of the Light, from the Desert to His Home ; and the Princes sing before Him a song of Triumph.

This was their Song :—" The Horse and his Rider Thou hast thrown into the Sea. The Leaders sank like stones to the bottom of the mighty waters. We sing to Thee for the greatness of Thy might. Thou art the strength, and praise, and gladness of Thy servants. Thy Right Hand hath slain the Dragon. In Thy wrath Thou hast swept away Thy enemies like stubble; with the blast of Thy nostrils they were destroyed. The waves were gathered together : the floods stood up in a heap. Thy foes sank as lead, and the deep waters covered them. Who is like to Thee among the strong, for Thy holiness and Thy wonders ? In Thy mercy Thou hast led Thy redeemed : in Thy strength Thou has brought them to Thy Home. The proud were troubled before Thee : they trembled and melted away. In the greatness of Thy Arm fear and dread fell upon them : they were immovable as a stone till Thy Brides passed by ; till the Ransomed passed by whom Thou hast loved. Thou hast carried Thy own, and hast set them to dwell on the Mountain of Thy inheritance ; in the Home which Thou hast made ready with Thy pierced Hands. Thou shalt reign for ever and ever. The Horse and his Rider Thou hast hurled into the Sea."

Their Hymn of Praise goes up in the Light like the sound of many waters.

Then the great silence thrills through that Home of Love, in which Jesus, God and Man, dwelleth for evermore.

Again go up the Alleluias of the Princes. Again the silence of the everlasting love thrills through the Garden of Lilies ; through the City and Paradise of God.

A Bride of the Crucified King has been brought back from the Darkness to the Light. Instead of ashes on her head she wears a Crown; and instead of sack-cloth she is clothed in the white Raiment of her Espousals. She has gone from the cavern of Dragons and the place of Creeping Things to her Father's House. The darkness has passed away for ever. In the everlasting gladness she lifts up her hands to God. She adores Him for evermore in His Temple ; and for evermore sees His Face.

EPILOGUE.

THE Morning Star shone, like a Beryl, in the sky, above the December snow. The air was clear and crisp overhead, and the snow was white and crisp under foot. Some trees stood up with leafless branches against the blue sky. All their bark and every twig on them were sparkling with Rhime. The broadly-spreading boughs of the firs bent downward beneath the covering that sheltered them from the cold.

The icicles hung from the rocks by the side of the swiftly-flowing River. Everywhere the white flakes glittered in the break of day.

Up and down the world the Corn lay safely hidden in the ground beneath that coverlet of snow.

The wrists of Winter were fastened with fetters of ice : and she wore a coronet of Cypress.

The breath of Spring, like the spell of an Enchantress, broke up the icy bands of the Winter, and went through the fastnesses of the cold. The world's heart was softened to its inmost depths at the sound of her voice. The snows melted; the white veil was taken from the earth; it was clothed in raiment of brown and green; and in a little while put on its many-coloured robe.

The tapering blades of the Corn shot up far above the ground.

In her hand Spring held a bunch of Hyacinths and Daffodils. On her head was a Primrose Crown.

Then Summer, coming after many days, walked in her majesty over the world. Her footprints were on the meadow and the hill. She dug in the Vineyards, dressing and pruning the Vines: she touched the Orchards with her hand and the Fruit began to ripen: she passed through the Cornfields, unlocking the garners of the earth. In the life-giving sunshine the wealth of the Year began to pour itself lavishly on the world.

The stalks, tall and graceful, lifted the green ears of Corn to the sun.

Summer looked on with a Lily for a Sceptre in her hand. She wore a garland of May.

The Corn shone in its golden beauty when

Autumn clothed herself in her jasper-like apparel. She carried a branch laden with Apples, and had a diadem of Sundews and Grass of Parnassus on her head. Far and near, between the hedgerows and against the dark-green thickets, there were gleams of that shining of the Corn.

The wheat was ready for the gathering, for the fields were white to the Harvest.

The Workers girded themselves and went down to the reaping. In the harvest-field their strong arms sent the sickles flashing through the yellow stalks. Swiftly the sheaves were bound; and the fields dotted with hooded Stooks.

The carts went onward to the Homestead: and the barns were soon filled with wealth. They were a sight of gladness, telling of food for the hungry and of the bread of man who goeth in the morning to his daily toil, and returneth from it beneath the shades of night. The heavy-laden carts went onward to the Homestead, through the lanes and beneath the trees. You could tell the way that they went by the stalks and heads of corn hanging in the branches among the leaves. The well-filled barns gave praise to the Lord of the Seasons, and the hearts of men were lifted up with joy.

O

There came a night on which a Supper was spread; and they who had reaped, and they for whom the reaping was done, gave thanks for the Corn that had been got in safely. The lamps were lighted, and the sound of music went up to the starry sky. It was the time when men rejoice in harvest, because of the goodness of the great Giver of all things. The songs of thankful gladness rose to His Ears from the Banquet girdled with garners that were filled with Corn and overflowing. With smiling face the night looked down upon the ingathering of the ripened grain.

The voice of praise, sweet and strong and piercing, went up through the Chestnuts and the Oaks and the Beeches, beyond the noise of the Waterfalls and the Sea, past the Night-wind and the glimmering of the Stars, from those who kept the Feast, with gladness of heart, in that great Day of the Harvest-Home.

PRINTED BY BALLANTYNE AND COMPANY
EDINBURGH AND LONDON

CHURCH MUSIC

PUBLISHED BY

BURNS, OATES, & CO.

LITURGICAL SERIES OF MASSES.

FOR GENERAL USE.

Now publishing, a new collection of MASSES, fitted in all respects for general Choir use. To suit the circumstances of different Churches, the music will be of two classes :

I.

EASY MASSES, chiefly for UNISON SINGING (which may also be sung alternately in parts), suited for smaller Choirs, or for week-day use in larger Churches ; also for Convent and College Chapels, &c. These Masses will have a full and artistic Organ Accompaniment, and will be so arranged that an effect will be produced scarcely inferior to that of Vocal Part Music.

II.

MASSES FOR FOUR VOICES, in the highest style of art, with Organ Obligato Accompaniment, by eminent composers. These Masses will be of full, without being of inconvenient, length ; and the Sanctus, Benedictus, &c., will in no case exceed the proper limits. These Masses will be arranged expressly for the present Series.

The Series is intended to embrace all the modern developments of musical art ; but at the same time regard will be had as to what is suitable for sacred, as distinguished from secular, use. As an additional guarantee it may be added that, in respect to the general character of the selection, as well as on the various points of detail, the "Instructions of the Holy See to Singers and Composers" will be taken by the Editors as their guide.

The whole will be under the supervision of professional musicians experienced in this department of art.

LONDON : BURNS, OATES, & CO., 17 PORTMAN STREET.

NEW SERIES OF SIX MASSES FOR FOUR VOICES.

*1. Mass of St. Stephen, for four voices, by J. N. Hummel.. 7s.
*2. Mass of St. Francis, 4 voices, by F. Schubert. 7s.
*3. Mass of St. Richard, 4 voices, by F. Seegner. 6s.
*4. Mass of St. Lucius, 4 voices, by V. Righini. 7s.
*5. Mass of St. Ferdinand, by F. Seegner. 6s.
*6. Mass of St. Edmund, by Danzi. 7s.

Vocal Parts, 1s. each Voice, or 4s. a set for each Mass.

FIRST SERIES.

*Mass of St. Charles, in E flat, by C. B. Witska. 5s.
*Mass in E flat, by C. L. Drobisch. 7s.
*Mass in D, by C. L. Drobisch. 7s.
*Mass in C, by F. Schneider. 7s.
*Mass in C, by S. Sechter. 7s.
*Mass in D, by Bernard Klein. 7s.
*Mass in A, by Casali. 5s. } Also suited for Advent and Lent.
*Mass in C, by Casali. 5s. }   See below (†).

A Series of easy Masses for Unison or Part-Singing is also published as follows :

*1. Mass of St. Edward, by Edward Fagan. 4s.
*2. Mass of St. John, by Arthur O'Leary. 4s.
*3. Mass of St. Vincent, by S. Sechter. 3s.
*4. Mass of St. Clement, by the same. 3s. 6d.
*5. Mass of St. Anselm, by J. Hallett Sheppard. 3s. 6d.
*6. Mass of St. Joseph, by Frederick Westlake. 5s.

MASSES FOR ADVENT AND LENT, FOR VOCAL PERFORMANCE.

*Casali's Mass of St. Felix, in A. 5s.†
*Casali's Mass of St. Victor, in C. 5s.†
*Casali's Mass of St. Bernard (a short Mass). 3s. 6d.
*Crookall's, John, D.D. (a short Mass). 3s. 6d.
*Palestrina's Mass, Eterna Christi munera. 3s. 6d.

*MOTETTS FOR ADVENT, FOR VOCAL PERFORMANCE.

1. Ad te levavi. 1s.—2. Deus tu convertens. 1s.—3. Benedixisti Domine. 1s.—4. Ave Maria. 1s.

*MOTETTS FOR LENT, FOR VOCAL PERFORMANCE.

1. Scapulis suis. 1s.—2. Meditabor. 1s.—3. Justitiæ Domini. 1s.—4. Laudate Dominum. 1s.—5. Confitebor tibi. 1s.—6. Palm

Sunday: Improperium. 1s.—Maundy Thursday: Dextera Domini. 1s.

MASSES FOR MEN'S VOICES.

Mass of St. Wilfrid, for two Tenors and two Basses, by J. Hallett Sheppard. 7s. 6d.
Mass for two Tenors and one Bass, by E. Kritschmer. 6s.
Mass for two Tenors and one Bass, by J. Lochmann. 6s.

SELECTIONS FROM HAYDN AND MOZART.

*1. Mass in B flat, by Haydn. Folio, 7s.—Voice parts, 1s. each.
*2. Mass in C, by Mozart. 7s.—Voice parts, 1s. each.

₌ These editions have the omitted words supplied, and the parts of undue length—such as the "Benedictus," &c.—brought within proper compass.

EASY MUSIC FOR THE INTROITS AND GRADUALS.

For Unison and Four Voices. 1s. 6d.
Words of the same, pointed to correspond. Cloth, 2s.

SHORT MOTETTS. Cheap and Easy Series.

1. Cœli enarrant. Marcello. 4 voices. 3d.
2. Sicut cervus. Marcello. 2 or 3 voices. 2d.
3. Sicut cervus. Gounod. 4 voices. 3d.—Also, for men's voices. 4 voices. 3d.
4. In te, Domine. Handel. 4 voices. 2d.
5. In te, Domine. Czerny. 4 voices. 3d.
6. In virtute tua. Marcello. 2 or 3 voices. 2d.
7. Meditabor. Casali. 4 voices. 3d.
8. Quam dilecta. Marcello. 2 voices. 2d.
9. Benedicam Dominum. Richardson. 4 voices. 3d.
10. Ave verum. Gounod. 5 voices. 3d.
11. Lætatus sum. Casali. 3 voices. 2d.
12. Ave Maria. Henry Smart. 4 voices. 6d.
13. Ave Maria. Sterndale Bennett. 4 voices. 6d.
14. Miserere. 4 voices. 1d.
15. Rorate cœli. 4 voices. 2d.
16. Adjuva nos. 4 voices. 1d.
17. Cibavit eos (men's voices). 3 voices. 1d.
18. Justorum animæ. Czerny. 4 voices. 1s.
19. Veni, Sponsa (men's voices). Baini. 3 voices. 6d.
20. Dominus firmamentum (men's voices). Terziani. 3 voices. 1s.

21. Panis angelicus. Palestrina. 4 voices. 1s.
22. Benedictus es. Czerny. 4 voices. 1s.
N.B. These Motetts are short, and would be suitable for filling
up the time after the proper words of the Offertory have been performed. Many of them may be sung without accompaniment.

EASY ANTIPHONS, HYMNS, &c.

23. Alma Redemptoris. Richardson and Witska. 4 voices. 4d.
24. Ave Regina. Romberg. 4 voices. 6d.
25. Regina cœli. O'Leary. 4 voices. 6d.
26. Salve Regina. Richardson. 4 voices. 3d.
27. Lauda Sion. O'Leary. 4 voices. 6d.
28. Veni, Sancte Spiritus. Schachner. 4 voices. 2d.
29. Victimæ Paschali. Waltaki. 4 voices. 3d.
30. Ave Maris Stella (4 various). 4 voices. 3d.
31. Adoro te devote, and Adoremus in æternum. 4 voices. 2d.
32. O filii et filiæ. Schachner. 4 voices. 4d.

PLAIN-CHANT MASSES.

*Ordinarium Missæ; all the Masses of the Roman Gradual,
with Accompaniment; 5s.

Missa de Angelis, 2s.; Voice Part, 6d.

*Requiem Mass (Roman), with Accompaniment, 3s.

Requiem Mass, Chant only, large type. Price 1s.; or done up
with cloth back, 1s. 6d.

Plain Chant Masses, harmonised by E. Fagan. Nos. 1, 2,
and 3, 1s. each; No. 4, 1s. 6d.; No. 5, 2s.

Missa in Solemnioribus, for 3 voices, by W. Boulvin. 4s. nett.

*N.B. Messrs. B. & Co. supply all Mass Music issued by other
publishers.*

MISCELLANEOUS MASSES.

Dr. Holloway's, 10s. 6d. | Roberti's, 12s.
F. Hermann's, 5s. | Cooke's, 8s.

Gounod's Messe de Ste. Cecile, 8vo, Score, 2s.
Ditto, with full Accompaniment for the Organ, 8s.
Messe des Anges, by S. Moorat, 12s.
Bordèse. Petite Messe solennelle, à deux voix. 3s.
Concone.   Do.   do.   2s. 6d.

HYMNS FOR THE FESTIVALS, &c. OF THE YEAR,

In Full Score, for Voices and Accompaniment; English Words.

1. Advent and Christmas, 6*d*.
2. The Holy Name, 6*d*.
3. Lent, and the Passion, 6*d*.
4. Easter and Ascension, 6*d*.
5. Whitsuntide, 6*d*.
6. Trinity, 6*d*.
7. All Saints and Heaven, 6*d*.
8. Hymns to our Saviour, 6*d*.
9. Hymns on the Christian Life, 6*d*.
10. Hymns of Praise, 6*d*.
11. Morning, 6*d*.
12. Evening, 6*d*.

NINE SHORT MOTETTS,

English and Latin Words,

For Two, Three, and Four Voices, by Casali, Marcello, Czerny, &c. 2*s*. ; or separately, as follow—

1. Cœli cnarrant,—(The heavens declare) (4 voices), Marcello; 3*d*.
2. Sicut cervus,*—(As the hart panteth) (2 or 3 voices), Marcello; 2*d*.
3. In virtute tua,*—(In Thy strength) (2 or 3 voices), Marcello; 2*d*.
4. In te Domine,—(In Thee, O Lord) (4 voices), Handel; 2*d*.
5. Meditabor in mandatis,—(I will meditate) (4 voices), Casali; 3*d*.
6. Quam dilecta*—(How lovely) (2 voices), Marcello; 2*d*.
7. Lætatus sum,—(I rejoiced) (3 voices), Casali; 2*d*.
8. Benedicam Dominum,—(I will bless) (4 voices), Richardson; 3*d*.
9. In te Domine,—(In Thee, O Lord) (Czerny) (4 voices); 3*d*.

* Suited chiefly for treble voices.

Sixteen Choice Part-Songs for Four Voices.

By MOLIQUE, MACFARREN, BENEDICT, BARNETT, WESTLAKE, &c. &c. 8vo, 2*s*. 6*d*.

SACRED PART-MUSIC BY B. MOLIQUE. Six Pieces. 1*s*. 6*d*.

SACRED PART-MUSIC BY SCHACHNER. Four Pieces. 8*d*.

SACRED PART-MUSIC BY MACFARREN. Four Pieces. 10*d*.

HYMNS, SACRED PART-SONGS, and other Pieces, by the best Composers; chiefly original. 8vo, red cloth, 12*s*.

This elegant volume contains 105 pieces, suited for public or private use, choral societies, &c.

[For other Music, see Complete List of Church Music by the same Publishers.]

HYMNS AND PART-SONGS, for Four Voices, or

Unison, with Accompaniment. Sold separately as follows:

The Pilgrims of the Night	*F. Westlake*	3d.
The hour of prayer	*B. Molique*	2d.
The eternal Summer	*Agnes Zimmermann*	2d.
The Land of Peace	*Frederick Westlake*	2d.
Come, O Creator Spirit (*Pentecost*)	*J. R. Schachner*	2d.
God my Rest	*Dr. E. G. Monk*	3d.
The shadows of the evening hours	*B. Molique*	3d.
Passing away	*G. A. Macfarren*	3d.
Departure	*B. Molique*	3d.
Like the voiceless starlight	*B. Molique*	2d.
The Prince of Peace (*Sacred Heart*)	*Jules Benedict*	2d.
Stars of glory (*Christmas*)	*Frederick Westlake*	3d.
O why art thou sorrowful	*W. Schulthes*	2d.
All ye who seek (*Sacred Heart*)	*G. A. Macfarren*	2d.
Sleep, holy Babe (*Christmas*)	*J. F. Barnett*	2d.
Expectation	*W. Schulthes*	2d.
O God, how wonderful Thou art	*J. R. Schachner*	2d.
Have mercy on us, God most high	*B. Molique*	2d.
God of mercy and compassion (*Lent*)	*B. Molique*	2d.
Jerusalem the Golden	*Dr. E. G. Monk*	1d.
Rest, weary soul	*G. Roberti*	3d.
Morning Prayer, and Fair was thy blossom	*Mendelssohn*	2d.
They whom we loved on earth	*Schachner*	2d.
Harvest Hymn	*Schachner*	1d.
I dwell a captive (*for Trebles*)	*Spohr*	1d.
He giveth His beloved sleep	*O'Leary*	2d.
Dear little One (*Christmas Cradle Song*)	*Roberti*	2d.
Christ the Lord is risen (*Easter*)	*Roberti*	2d.
Evening Hymn	*Macfarren*	2d.
O'erwhelmed in depths of woe (*Lent*)	*Macfarren*	2d.
Laud, O Sion, thy salvation (*Lauda Sion*)	*O'Leary*	3d.
Pilgrims of the Night (Hark, hark, my soul)	*Richardson*	1d.
O Paradise (*Two Melodies*)	*Barnett, &c.*	1d.
Sweet Saviour, bless us (*Two Melodies*)	*Westlake and G. H.*	1d.
The Precious Blood of Jesus (*Two Hymns*)	*Do. do.*	1d.
My Shepherd is the living God	*Spohr*	1d.
Jesus, the only thought of Thee	*Richardson*	1d.

Each free by post for an extra stamp.

Pieces to the value of a Shilling free for 12 stamps.

NEW, CHEAP, AND COMPREHENSIVE COLLECTION OF

𝕸𝖚𝖘𝖎𝖈 𝖋𝖔𝖗 𝕮𝖍𝖚𝖗𝖈𝖍 𝕮𝖍𝖔𝖎𝖗𝖘,

Containing 230 pieces.

··· -

THE

POPULAR CHOIR MANUAL,

Rendering easy for the least experienced Choir the Music for the Year.

In one handsome Volume, cloth, price 10s. 6d., or in Two Parts

PART I. THE MORNING OFFICES.

Price 3s. 6d.

Previous to the present Publication, there existed no work containing a complete collection, in regular order, of all the Music to be performed in the Morning Offices of the Church throughout the year. One book contained one thing ; another, another ; but it needed a dozen different publications to supply the want of choirs ; and even then many things were deficient, while others were printed in such a way as to be unintelligible to ordinary singers. It is hoped that the present attempt to supply the desideratum will be found of practical utility.

Besides the usual music for the *Asperges, Vidi Aquam, Responses,* &c., an easy arrangement of Chants has been given, by means of which the *Introits* and *Graduals*—those characteristic parts of the Service of the day, which should never be omitted except through necessity—can be performed, even by the least experienced choir.

Next, there are the whole of the "HOLY WEEK SER-VICES," from Palm Sunday to Holy Saturday inclusive, arranged and printed so that they can be sung by any choir without the possibility of mistake. The text of the Music is taken from the most approved sources ;—while Chants are adapted to the *Graduals, Tracts,* &c., where the Ritual Music would be too long and difficult. In a similar way has been given the Office for *Candlemas-day.*

Music in various attractive forms for the four *Sequences* of the year, followed by the *Te Deum* and several miscellaneous pieces, completes this portion of the work.

PART II. THE EVENING OFFICES.

Price 5s. 6d.

This Part forms a complete Guide and Manual for Organist and Choir. It contains eight times the amount of matter of "Webbe's Motetts," and all the pieces are such as are really wanted.

Among the contents are the whole series of *Vesper Hymns*, in every variety of setting; the "*Magnificat*" and *Psalm Tones*, in an entirely novel and lucid arrangement; the four *Antiphons* of the Blessed Virgin in great variety; upwards of thirty "*O Salutaris*" and "*Tantum Ergo;*" a choice selection of *Litanies*, and a large variety of *Hymns, Antiphons*, and other Pieces for *Benediction;* also the Music for the "*Bona Mors;*" Hauptmann's "*Salve Regina*," and many other favourite pieces sung by the Farm-Street Choir.

The Pieces in this Part, if published separately, in the usual size, would not amount to less than 8l. or 10l.

BRIEF SYNOPSIS OF CONTENTS OF THE WORK.

*** *A variety of settings are given for each piece.*

PART I.

MORNING.—Asperges—Vidi aquam—Introits—Graduals—Responses—Benedicamus—Domine salvam—Victimæ Paschali—Veni Sancte—Lauda Sion—Stabat Mater—Purification—Palm Sunday—Good Friday—Holy Saturday—Litanies—Confirmation—Te Deum.

PART II.

EVENING.— Order of Vespers— Directions for Chanting—Compline—Benediction — Magnificat in tabular form for the 8 tones—Psalm tones and their endings—Hymns at Vespers (52)—Alma—Ave Regina—Regina cœli—Salve Regina—Hæc dies—Rorate cœli—Adjuva nos—Adeste fideles—O filii et filiæ—Adoro te devote—Adoremus in æternum—Ave verum—Tota pulchra—De profundis—Miserere—O salutaris (24)—Tantum ergo (15)—Litanies (55)—Bona Mors.

*** *The Morning and Evening Offices in one Volume, strongly bound in cloth, lettered, price* 10s. 6d.

A considerable reduction to Choirs taking six or more copies.